Jack Boyz N Da Bronx 2

Romell Tukes

Lock Down Publications and Ca$h
Presents

Jack Boyz N Da Bronx 2

A Novel by *Romell Tukes*

Romell Tukes

Lock Down Publications
P.O. Box 944
Stockbridge, Ga 30281
www.lockdownpublications.com

Copyright 2021 by Romell Tukes
Jack Boyz N Da Bronx 2

Lock Down Publications
Like our page on Facebook: Lock Down Publications @
www.facebook.com/lockdownpublications.ldp
Book interior design by: **Shawn Walker**
Edited by: **Tamira Butler**

Stay Connected with Us!

Text **LOCKDOWN** to 22828 to stay up-to-date with new releases, sneak peaks, contests and more...
Thank you!

Submission Guideline.

Submit the first three chapters of your completed manuscript to ldpsubmissions@gmail.com, subject line: Your book's title. The manuscript must be in a .doc file and sent as an attachment. Document should be in Times New Roman, double spaced and in size 12 font. Also, provide your synopsis and full contact information. If sending multiple submissions, they must each be in a separate email.

Have a story but no way to send it electronically? You can still submit to LDP/Ca$h Presents. Send in the first three chapters, written or typed, of your completed manuscript to:

LDP: Submissions Dept
P.O. Box 944
Stockbridge, Ga 30281

DO NOT send original manuscript. Must be a duplicate.

Provide your synopsis and a cover letter containing your full contact information.

Thanks for considering LDP and Ca$h Presents.

Acknowledgements

First and foremost, all praise due to Allah because I'm nothing without him. Thank you to all my readers for the support; we litty y'all. Big shout to my hood, Yonkers, NY, Mount Vernon, and 914 as a whole. Shout Moreno the bro, CB, YB, SG, Lingo, Banger, Brisco, Kazzy. Shout my Brooklyn guys, Rico-Flatbush, OG Chuck, Tim Dog, DayDay-Crown Heights, and Tails, free da bro. My BX guys, the Hats, The G's, Uptown to da South Bronx, Patterson Pjs, Burnside-Dru. And Staten Island, free Dex and Free. Shout Bum from L.I. Shout to my NJ and Philly guys. Shout to my Atlanta Zone 6 nigga and my Miami and NC guys. Big shout to Ca$h and LDP; we shaking the building. The game is ours. Thanks to all editors and hard workers making this shit happen. Stay tuned. Stay focused and positive. Free all the real, this prison shit ain't worth it or nothing to glorify. Live life, raise a family. Some people won't ever have that chance again. Raise above the barrier set before us and sky's the limit. Thank you.

Romell Tukes

Prologue

6 Months Ago

Knight and his crew were running around the Bronx streets robbing any nigga who was getting to a bag. As their names started to ring around the city, karma was starting to catch up with the Bronx natives.

When they robbed a drug lord by the name of Fats, the city turned into a war zone. Fats' worker, Glock, from Soundview Projects, had problems with Knight and his friend, D Fatal Brim, long before they jacked his connect, Fats. After killing Glock's baby mother, D Fatal Brim was locked up by the feds and sentenced to life in prison.

Glock paid YG and his brother, PG, to take care of Knight, Kazzy, Kip Loc, Paco, Black, and Less, but instead, it backfired. Once Glock killed Knight and Kazzy's little brother, Kip Loc, in a club, Kazzy turned up while Knight moved to VA with his uncle Slim who was plugged in with a Kingpin named Gotti.

While Knight was in VA chasing a big bag, so was Kazzy in the BX, but the blood spill was getting worse, especially when Black's mom got killed. Black was Knight and Kazzy's best friend, and his mom raised them in MillBrook Projects. She was a cop.

When PG and his mother got murdered, YG went crazy. Glock's best friend, Bankroll, was also coming for Kazzy and the crew's heads.

Knight ended up robbing a big-time plug named CL, who was his uncle Slim's connect's brother. Meanwhile, Knight met Gotti's sister, Stephen, who he started fucking and doing business with because she was a plug also.

One night, Gotti called Uncle Slim and Knight to his VA mansion to tell them he heard someone was working with the feds trying to build a case on them. Everybody was shocked, but when Gotti said who it was, Knight was shocked to hear his uncle Slim was a rat.

Gotti made Knight kill his own uncle right there that night. Months later, Knight ended up robbing Gotti and killing his goons while Gotti went into a panic room, watching Knight's every move through a double mirror. It wasn't too long after Knight robbed Gotti that he ended up getting set up by his man. Knight got caught with a key of coke and a gun, sending him to jail. While in jail, he was stabbed up by a few prisoners in his cell, but luckily, another prisoner from Bad News, VA came to his aid.

Meanwhile, Knight's mom was killed by Glock, and months later, Glock was killed by Knight and Kazzy Loc's little brother, Lil' K. Lil' K and his crew were robbing drug dealers all around the Bronx, even his own brother's spots. When Lil' K kidnapped Less and made Kazzy get his friend from a warehouse, the brothers had a long talk about taking over the city's drug trade and jacking any crew in the way.

The two crews formed a power bond but agreed to do their own thing and stay outta each other's way. Kazzy was still mad at Lil' K for robbing his spot, and Less was mad at all of them for kidnapping him. This was a new chapter in the BX.

Chapter 1

Lamburg Projects, BX

Randy had been in his projects all day, trappin' hard on the first of the month. He made 30,000 in a whole day of hustling. This was Randy's hood, born and raised.

He was selling drugs for Big Blazer, his big homie, who had Soundview on lock since Glock got murdered. Moving ten keys a week was nothing compared to most hustlers who were big time, but to Randy, he was that nigga.

It was 8 p.m. and he ran outta work, so he went in his building where he kept his stash in his little cousin's apartment. He was trying to make another 10K before he called it a night and went to his baby mother's crib on West Farms next to the Bronx Zoo.

"Yo, Randy, what's up? Let me get some credit nigga, I'm your uncle," Randy's uncle Playa said, coming out the build with his ashy face and missing teeth.

"Uncle, not right now, please, and you still owe me three hundred dollars, and you coming out the trap," Randy told him, seeing the smirk on his uncle's face.

"You caught me, nephew, but I'm about to get clean. I'm tryna get some money."

"I got you when you get clean, but I gotta go," Randy stated, walking off.

Upstairs, Randy made his way down the hall to the last apartment. Before going inside, the next door apartment door opened and three niggas stepped out with guns, holding him at gunpoint.

"Go inside," Lil' K told him, as the silencer attached to his Glock was screwed on the tip of the pistol.

"Aight, bro..." Randy's whole body was shaking, stepping into the apartment to see his cousin in the kitchen cooking dinner.

PSST, PSST, PSST!

Banger shot Randy's cousin in her neck, killing her instantly.

"Take me to the money and drugs, and I ain't got no time for games," Lil' K told Randy, who was crying.

"Ok... I swear, it's all yours, son. I'm just trying to make it home to my kids," Randy cried, in tears.

Randy went into the back room and pulled out a duffle bag full of money and bricks.

"This is it, bro." Randy passed over his life savings.

"Thanks."

PSST...

PSST...

PSST...

PSST...

Lil' K put four in the back of his head after taking the bag.

"We litty, son," Lil' K told Banger and Bugatti Boy before walking out the apartment.

***

Hunts Point, Bronx

Kazzy Loc, Paco, and Less were in the warehouse waiting for the meeting with Lil' K's crew to go over the terms of their agreement. In the last six months, Lil' K and his crew had been going crazy in the streets, robbing and killing everything.

Kazzy Loc had been focused on money and taking over the streets. Kazzy had a new girl, and her father was a plug in the Dominican Republic.

"Yo, son, where these little niggas at?" Paco said, checking his bust-down AP watch.

"They coming, bro," Less stated.

"Factz," Kazzy said as the warehouse doors opened and Lil' K and his crew walked inside dressed in all black.

Less laughed and Kazzy gave him a look, because he knew how Lil' K was. Kazzy also knew Less was still upset about them kidnapping him. If Lil' K wasn't Kazzy's little brother, he would have been killed him and his whole crew.

Lil' K had Banger, Blu, Red, and Bugatti Boy behind him.

"What's goody, bro?" Lil' K said, standing in front of his older brother. "You know what's good, son, y'all niggas making the city hot, bro. Y'all killed four niggas from my block because a nigga ain't wanna give you his re-up money. You tryna risk your life for chump change. I got work, so let me put you on, son. We already paved the way for y'all, facts," Kazzy told Lil' K, only to see him laugh.

"Nigga, we self-made, bro. I don't need shit from you or your soft ass crew. This my family, and we gonna get it how we live, son. I bet that, and whoever—"

"Wooh, hold on, fam, before this shit go left. I respect you as a man, and if you wanna crash out in these streets, then do you, but I'ma tell you this, boy. You may have some little dirty niggas in your circle, but real family always gonna be in your corner." Kazzy Loc walked out on that with his crew behind.

Less mean mugged all of them before walking out.

"Man, fuck this, I say we—"

"Nigga, shut the fuck up," Lil' K cut off Banger, because he knew he was about to say some dumb shit.

"Let's get out of here," Red said, fixing her long hair she had in a ponytail. She knew Lil' K was pissed right now, she could see it on his face. She knew him better than she knew herself.

Romell Tukes

Chapter 2

Michell Projects, Bronx

Lil' K and Red were in the back of projects where Red and Banger lived.

"This shit out here moving," Lil' K said, seeing fiens running from build to build copping crack from their crew.

Red and Banger formed a crew of young niggas who sold G-packs for them, which was a thousand dollars' worth of drugs. Outta the thousand dollars, they took a 60 and 40 perfect, leaving them with four hundred dollars for themselves.

"Yeah, we moving a quarter brick a day. That's dealing with crackheads, but what we gonna do when we run out?" Red asked, looking at her best friend to see he had no answer whatsoever.

"I'ma figure something out, just give me some time, sis."

Lil' K got a call from Bugatti Boy, forgetting he had to go to Jackson Projects to meet him.

"I already know, but call me later. I got a question before you go," she said

"What's poppin', Red?"

"Do you think we can trust Kazzy and them niggas? Because I didn't trust the way he was looking at you."

Red had been waiting to tell Lil' K how she really felt about his brother, but since their mother was killed, Lil' K's brothers were all he had. Even though Lil' K didn't fuck with his brothers, they were still his blood, and Red understood that.

"Trust has nothing to do with understanding the terms of our agreement we made with them. They gonna respect our shit and we gonna respect theirs, sis. Any lines get crossed, we handle our business," Lil' K said sternly.

"Ok, but I don't trust or like that Less nigga. He do anything funny, I'ma send him to the most high," she told him, seeing him laugh before walking off.

Red walked into her building and took the elevator to the sixth floor, where she lived with her mom and brother, Banger, who was in Albany with Blu. Her mom was at work, so she had the crib to herself. Red was eighteen now and wanted her own spot. She hated living with her mom and brother. Her older sister moved out after she got married to some nerd nigga who worked for a computer tech company. Red laid in her bed, taking off her new pair of Jordan sneakers. She had a closet full of new sneakers and fly designer clothes. Red dressed like a tomboy but with a girly swag. She was bi-sexual but mainly into girls, because when she was younger, her father raped her, and she'd never been the same since around males.

The only one she felt comfortable around was Lil' K, who was her best friend since the sandbox. She also fucked with Blu and Bugatti Boy. They were like family to her. A lot of guys tried to holler at Red because she was a dime, with light skin, colorful eyes, and long hair dropping to her butt.

Red got on social media checking her IG account on her iPhone, looking at all the likes her pics with her crew got in the club last night.

***

Big Blazer had five dancers in his VIP shaking their asses as his crew tossed money over the floor. Today was Big Blazer's birthday, so he was turning up with his crew from Soundview Projects.

Since Big Blazer came home from prison a half a year ago, he'd been taking over the city drug trades. With Fats as a plug, he was unstoppable. He basically took his best friend Glock's spot in the streets. When Big Blazer heard about Glock's murder, he was sick and wanted blood, but first he had to rebuild his own empire and get his money right.

His crew, Holiday, 45, Head, and Bags, was his family, day-one niggas. They would do anything for the big homie. Big Blazer was like a Suge Knight to the hood, in Southview. He was labeled to soon be one of the biggest kingpins coming out of the Bronx.

Everything wasn't peaches and cream, because recently, one of his spots got robbed, and he wanted answers. There were only two crews in the BX running around robbing shit, and one was Kazzy Loc and his crew. Big Blazer heard of another crew of young niggas from the South Bronx robbing shit also. He put his goons on them to see what they came up with.

"Yo, son, these hoes tryna slide," 45 told Big Blazer, sipping out a bottle of D'ussé.

"Go ahead, Blood, you and Head do y'all, son. Me, Holiday, and Bags going out to that new strip joint in Long Island," Big Blazer told 45.

"Copy, bro, love you. Happy B Day, son," 45 said, hugging Big Blazer's wide frame.

"Yo, Head, you drive, son. This nigga gone off that D'ussé." Big Blazer laughed at 45, who almost fell when he stood up.

"I'm 'bout to take this nigga home to his BM, son," Head said, helping 45.

Once Head took 45 home, the rest of the gang went club hopping to enjoy Big Blazer's birthday. He loved hitting the clubs, so he could stunt on niggas. He called himself the King of New York. Big Blazer wished his little brother Lil' Blazer was here, but he was on his way home in a couple of months from Sing-Sing prison.

Chapter 3

Sux2 Prison, VA

Knight was in one of the wildest prisons in VA. He was in a high maximum-security prison where niggas were dying weekly. Luckily, Knight ran into a lot of niggas from New York in the jail, so he was in good company.

Last month, Knight cut a nigga in his face for disrespecting him in front of prisoners in the dorm. He was in the special housing unit, which was the box. Knight was in the cell doing push-ups in reps of fifty, trying to do 2500.

Being locked in a cell all day did something to most prisoners, but Knight loved his solitary away from population.

He was sentenced to two years in prison for a gun and a key of coke. His first offer was five years, but he had the best lawyer in VA. Stephen provided him with a lawyer because he held it down where he could have snitched on her, but he didn't.

Knight wrote Kazzy last week telling him to go to Miami to meet Stephen. Knight didn't want Kazzy out there risking his life for pennies when he could be getting big money and locking down the streets of the Bronx.

Being incarcerated gave Knight a different way of thinking and a better outlook on life itself. He was so used to being a jack boy, he felt like that was all he knew, until speaking to older brothers who were stuck in prison for life for the same life he was living. Knight learned a lot from other prisoners. Some were successful millionaires, while others were kingpins and killers.

After working out, he took a bird bath in the sink while waiting on his last meal at 3:30 p.m. The food sucked in the SHU, but Knight had no choice but to eat the slop.

He lost some good time and was sentenced to 90 days in the box, but he still got visits from Mita, who was a young, beautiful DA in VA. But she told him at the end of the year she was moving back to New York, because she didn't fit in VA. The court system was unfair and very racist.

***

Manhattan, NY

Jacqueline worked overnight as a security guard in a fancy building made for millionaires, or people with a high income who lived an upscale lifestyle. Jacqueline was a nice looking Spanish woman in her early twenties. She was one of Paco's sisters—his favorite sister at that.

Every thirty minutes, she walked around the outside of the tall build that had twenty-nine floors. She was tired and ready to get back home to her four-month-old daughter her baby father was watching. Having a baby was harder than she thought, but she was lucky to have a good baby father, and Paco was taking care of her.

Last week, Paco bought her a new car. She loved her brother, but she didn't want to see him in prison like everybody else who did dirt. Jacqueline wasn't green. She knew what Paco did in the streets, and she prayed he would give up his dangerous lifestyle.

She got up from the lobby desk and went to make her rounds outside first, then she planned to check each floor. Outside, it was windy tonight. She wished she would have grabbed her sweater from inside. Normally, there were two people on duty, but her coworker called out sick tonight, leaving her all alone.

Jacqueline thought she heard something behind her, but before she could turn around, a man put her in a chokehold. Bankroll choked the life outta her then snapped her neck, killing her, and tossed her light body.

***

Bankroll climbed back into his black Range, getting on the FBR highway on his way back to Mount Vernon where he'd been recently staying. Last week, Bankroll got out of rehab, and he was on a mission to finish what he started with Kazzy, Paco, Less, and Black, who he heard was hiding out in some witness protection shit.

Bankroll had a bad drug habit before going to rehab, but now he got himself together and was back in full effect. He knew to play the shadows and wait until it was time to hop out and kill again, but for now, he was going back to Mount Vernon to his girlfriend he met at rehab.

***

Harlem, NY

YG walked out of Wagner Projects where he'd been living since moving out the Bronx after beefing with Knight and Kazzy's crew. He lost everything he loved to them when they were at war. Moving to Harlem, he met a beautiful Spanish chick and gave her a seed. Luckily, she had a good job while YG played the crib most of the time.

YG still was cautious as he always looked over his shoulder. The other day, he received a letter from his man Lil' Blazer, who was uptop telling him he had big plans for when he touched soon. Every day, YG thought about Kazzy and his gang. He wanted revenge, but he had no money, no guns, no army, or no help, but he knew his time would come again.

Romell Tukes

Chapter 4

Washington Ave, BX

Zendaya was Bugatti Boy's girlfriend of six months, but there was a lot of shit he didn't know about his girl. He had no clue Bankroll was her half-brother—they had the same father. Bugatti Boy loved her slim frame and high-yellow skin with her chinky eyes. Zendaya was eye candy, but she was all for Bugatti Boy.

He had his rod deep into her tightness as he fondled her small breasts and kissed her soft lips, making love to her.

"Uhhhggg . . . shhhhh . . mmm . . ." Zendaya moaned, giving out a long groan, pushing her hips forward.

She wrapped her legs around his body, clenching her sex muscles, making him go crazy.

"I'm about to let off," he said before cuming inside of her.

Zendaya wanted to ride, that was her favorite position. She got in her man's lap, slowly lowering herself onto his pole. Her body spasmed while his pipe disappeared inside of her as she began to yelp. The dick felt so good in her, she started her own rhythm as she bounced up and down as if a rap song played in her mind.

Bugatti felt like he was about to cum again, so he tried to slow her down. He wasn't about to let her put him to shame tonight. The good thing he loved about her was she could fuck for hours.

"I love you, Bugatti," she moaned, poppin' her ass on his dick until she climaxed. "You staying home, daddy?" Zendaya asked, climbing out the California king-size bed to put on her robe to go check on her one-year-old son she had with her ex, who was in prison serving 40 years.

"I'ma be back in the morning, baby," Bugatti told her, getting dressed, seeing it was only 10 pm, but he had to go meet Lil' K across town.

"When are you gonna ever spend a whole night with your woman instead of running the streets, Bugatti? You gotta grow up," Zendaya told him before walking out the room.

Bugatti paid her no mind, because she wasn't talking that shit when she was just riding his dick, so he didn't want to hear it.

Bugatti left his crib and made his way to the meet-up spot where Lil' K was waiting for him. Lil' K had an easy lick for them tonight in Yonkers. Lil' K told him about it the other day, but tonight, they were putting it in motion.

***

Yonkers, NY
One Hour Later

"Bro, who hides money in a barber shop?" Bugatti asked Lil' K, walking to the barber shop on the corner.

The owner of the shop was a big-time weed and ecstasy dealer. Every night, he left the shop with $50,000 or more. He had workers selling his product, and he was selling weight out of his shop.

"A damn nigga. This is a life lesson (laughs), facts, brotty, but we need a big lick, son. I'm starting to feel like we out here in the way. Yeah, MillBrook and Michell pjs doing a little numbers, but I want more," Lil' K said, being honest.

"Like Kazzy and them?" Bugatti knew Lil' K like the back of his hand, and he always wanted to be like his brothers.

"No, I want us to have our own and be our own, bro. Fuck them niggas, son. We gotta focus on us, fam, word up," Lil' K stated.

"Bro, I think you should have let Kazzy help us with a plug at least, bro. Who wants to rob goofy niggas all day? We seeing a little money, but if we find a plug, we'll be up," Bugatti made a point.

"Fuck that shit . . . ."

"You gotta put your pride to the side, dog, and bottle up your emotions," Bugatti told him.

"There he go right there . . ." Lil' K hopped out with his weapon on deck, seeing Sazon walk to his car with a bookbag.

Bloc . . .
Bloc . . .
Bloc . . .
Lil' K shot Sazon in his leg, dropping him where he stood. Bugatti took the bookbag off his shoulders and looked inside to see stacks of money in rubber bandz. "Ahhhhhhh!" Sazon held his bleeding leg, almost in tears. When Bugatti gave Lil' K a head nod letting him know the money was there, Lil' K shot Sazon twice in the face. They drove back to the Bronx, seconds away, $60,800 richer, but they always divided their profits.

***

Bridgeport, CT

Dollar looked at his wife laying in bed asleep. He closed the bedroom door behind him as he went to make himself a cup of coffee. Dollar took his meds every morning for his PTSD he got from being in the army overseas fighting in the war.

He was thirty-six years old and on his second marriage because he truly abhorred being single and lonely. His first wife, Mauda, was killed by Paco and his people. Dollar was Glock's older brother, who spent 15 years in the army, but he was back and back for blood.

When Glock told him he needed some help, he sent his wife, Mauda, who was a trained gun specialist. He thought Mauda would get the job done in a matter of days, but he ain't know she was going to fall in love.

Dollar was tall, chiseled, bald headed, and handsome. Nobody would be able to tell he's a cold-blooded killer. The last few months, he'd been planning on how he was gonna handle Kazzy, Paco, Less, and the other kid who fell off the face of the Earth.

Dollar had some good connections to computer hackers and gun suppliers who were overseas with him but were now back in New York. He could find the life story on a nigga in five seconds.

Today, Dollar was going to New York, a place he hadn't been since Glock's funeral, but he had to see what he was about to be up against.

Chapter 5

Manhattan, NY

Lil' Blazer had only been in the free world for 12 hours, and he was already in the club popping bottles. He just came home from doing a bid in Clinton Maximum Security Prison. Lil' Blazer was a Blood gang member. He was a Blood Hound, so he and his crew were running around the prison cutting other rivals in the face.

The club was poppin' tonight. Women were everywhere, and so were haters. Lil' Blazer came home to $200,000, his own condo, and an all-red Benz coupe.

Lil' Blazer brought out ten niggas with him and his man YG, who he kept in touch with while he was up north. When the two men met on Rikers Island, they formed a strong bond and respect for each other.

"Yo, son, I'm glad you home, bro, but what's your plan?" YG asked Lil' Blazer, who was sitting back on the couch enjoying the whole club scene, because before he went in, he was too young to hit clubs, but now, at the age of 21, he was living life.

"I'm about to get to this bag, fam. You know how I'm about to shake the streets, son, big facts," Lil' Blazer protested.

"The streets ain't the same no more," YG told him.

"So I heard, but me and my crew about to turn shit up in the Bronx, son. They got a crew I'm looking forward to coming across real soon, well, two crews. Niggas named Kazzy Loc and Lil' K."

When Lil' Blazer said them niggas, YG felt his heart race.

Just hearing Kazzy's name brought chills to his body.

"I know them very well," YG stated.

"Oh shit, how?"

"I was beefing with them niggas, bro. They killed my family," YG said in a sad voice.

"Damn, bro, I'm sorry to hear that, but we can team up and get these niggas back. Your name speaks for itself in the city, bro, but my brother the plug. We need you on the squad, bro," Lil' Blazer stated.

"I just had a seed, but let me sleep on it, bro. I got a lot going on right now," YG stated.

"I feel you, bro, I'm here."

Lil' Blazer saw the sexy bottle girls bring four bottles of D'ussé over while he listened to Lil' Baby's new song play in the club speakers.

***

Harlem, NY
Meanwhile

Vickie was in her crib feeding her baby while her baby father, YG, was out in a club doing whatever he was doing. Vickie was a beautiful Spanish woman who was the daughter of a well-known judge. Once she had a baby, her mom cut her off because she knew YG was a criminal and a thug.

Vickie was making the baby's bottle when she heard a knock at the door. She knew that was YG's dirty ass, and she couldn't wait to curse him out.

"You know—" Vickie started to shout when she opened the door, only to see two guns pointed at her.

"Bitch, get the fuck inside!" Paco shouted, pushing her inside.

Less closed the door behind him and walked inside.

"Please, my child is sleep...don't hurt me!" she screamed, seeing this type of shit on TV.

"Bitch, where is YG?" Paco asked.

"He's out at a club. Please, I have nothing to do with whatever is going on, please!" she screamed out loudly.

"Call him," Less told her, looking at her phone on the counter.

***

Manhattan, NY

YG was on his way out the club when he heard his phone going off non-stop. He knew it was Vickie blowing up the phone, as always. Every time he went out to a club, or even to the store, she would stalk his line.

Vickie was a good girl, in college trying to become a lawyer when he met her, but once they started dating and having sex, she got pregnant. After getting pregnant, her mom got her a job as a court clerk and cut her off.

"Vickie, I'm on my way home. I hate when you do this lame shit!" he shouted as he walked to his car.

All he heard were her cries, which was rare, because she never cried.

"Baby, what's wrong?"

"They here looking for you, YG!" she shouted.

"Who?" YG said, hearing someone take the phone.

"Nigga, I'm backkkkkkkk," Less said through the phone.

"I'ma kill you, nigga!" YG screamed into the phone, then chuckled.

"Aight, my G, I'll see you then." *BOOM!* "You heard that, bitch nigga? That was your bitch, and this is your seed, fuck nigga." *BOOM . . . Click . . .*

When the phone hung up, YG got weak in his knees, falling to the floor. When he got on his feet, he got in his car, racing to Harlem, praying Less was faking.

Romell Tukes

Chapter 6

Waymart, PA

D Fatal Brim was locked up in Canaan USP Maximum Security Prison. He was serving his life sentence. Since he blew trial, he'd been waiting to hear back on his direct appeal from the second circuit court of appeals. He'd been in the law library lately focusing on his case, because the judge railroaded him without any hardcore evidence.

D Fatal Brim was in his unit on the top tier in the corner, exercising. He was doing 500 burpees and jumping jacks. After his cardio routine, he planned to do some pull-ups in the shower on the pipe since the unit didn't have a pull-up bar or dip bar.

He normally did dips off the rail of the stairs. He hated the prison because most of the prisoners were fresh in and their first time in prison, so they were running around like madmen. Last week, D Fatal Brim had to beat one of his homies in the cell because he owed him twenty dollars, but for D Fatal Brim, it was the principle.

His brother, Less, came to see him twice and he always sent money. Kazzy Loc always wrote and sent money. Paco sent two bitches to see him, and he sent some drugs with them, so D Fatal Brim had the prison going crazy with the drug flow. He had all the Blood homies on the yard eating good. Niggas loved D Fatal Brim for what he could do for them.

When his two-hour work-out was done, two white boys stopped him, asking for 300 dollars' worth of drugs on credit until their girlfriends got their income tax. D Fatal Brim looked at them as if they were joking, before walking off to his cell to prepare for his shower.

He called one of his young homies to post up outside the shower on guard duty. After his shower, he planned to go outside to the yard to holler at his boy, Burn, from Long Island.

***

Santo Domingo, DR

Kazzy and his little Dominican bitch, Ulissa, just landed in DR. They were in a cab driving through the city part of Santo Domingo. "It's nice, huh, papi?" Ulissa asked in her deep Spanish accent. She was born and raised in Santo Domingo.

Ulissa moved to New York five years ago, when she turned eighteen, for a better life. She started dancing to pay for college, which she ended up dropping out anyway once she got a good job working for a modeling agency.

She was drop-dead gorgeous, but her only issue was she didn't have an ass or big breasts. This was why she was in DR, to get her body done at the expense of her boyfriend, who she'd been dealing with for two months now. She fell hard for Kazzy. He had that street vibe and he was good to her, unlike most men, who just wanted a fuck.

"I can't wait until I introduce you to my family, and don't be looking at my mom; she looks younger than me," she said laughing, staring out the window at the tourist spots.

"Maybe I need to bring her back to the states." Kazzy smiled as she hit his arm.

Kazzy loved spending time with Ulissa. Not only was she sexy, but she was down to earth. The vibe they shared was special. They met in a fast food restaurant, and it was history ever since.

Kazzy had never been outta the streets, but he was loving DR. He wished his goons were here, but they were trapping hard.

Kazzy got a call from a woman named Stephen, who said she was a good friend of Knight's and would be pleased if he came to Miami so they could talk. He agreed, because he already knew who she was. Knight told him about her in so many words.

The cab pulled up at a large, fancy hotel with a beach in the back area on a private island. Kazzy and Ulissa went to the room and had a mean fuck session. They were both so horny from the long flight, so it was on and poppin'.

***

Sing-Sing Prison, NY

Bankroll was parked outside the prison watching for his boy, Factz, to come out. Factz was Bankroll's childhood friend who'd been locked up since he was eighteen, and now he was 30 years old. He saw the big, black, ugly nigga with the missing front tooth approaching him, smiling.

"What up, little nigga?" Factz bear hugged his boy.

"What's poppin', Blood, welcome home. Let's get away from these gates, bro. I got two bad bitches waiting on you right now, son," Bankroll said, seeing his phone light up.

"Oh, yeah? Well, let's get the fuck outta here, fam," Factz said, excited to release 12 years of hardship.

Romell Tukes

Chapter 7

Edenwald Projects, BX

YG was back in the Bronx in full effect. He recently started fucking with Lil' Blazer, and he had the bricks on deck, so he gave ten keys to YG to get him back in the game. In the last couple of days, YG had been in Mott Haven with his young boys trying to put them on some money. He was parked in the back of the Edenwald Projects where fifty Bloods were posted up, rolling dice and selling drugs, regular Bronx shit.

"Where the fuck is this nigga at?" YG said to himself, watching the exit door.

Ten seconds later, the back door opened and his uncle Mikey stepped up. Uncle Mikey was an ex-fiend who knew how to get money when he was clean off drugs. He was a legend in Edenwald because he killed two police in the stairwell before they installed cameras there. He ended up beating the bodies.

YG saw his uncle coming his way and shook his head, watching him walk with a limp like he was a real pimp.

"YG, what's poppin', youngin'? I see you out here looking real smooth in this BMW spaceship. Back in my day, I used to have something like this," Uncle Mikey said, chewing on a toothpick, which he always did.

"This sumthin' lite, fam, but how's everything?" YG asked.

"Good, I'm sorry about what happened to your mom, bro, and sis, may Allah bless their souls. I heard you was outta town somewhere hidden," Uncle Mikey said with his loose lips. One thing about Mikey, he was the type to say anything out his mouth.

"Whoever told you that, tell them to suck my dick wit' their mother's lips. I never ran from no nigga. My body count speaks for itself," YG shot back.

"Calm down, nephew, I'm on your team. I know how you get down, baby boy," Uncle Mikey stated.

"I had a seed and was in Harlem, but them niggas stole my family," YG said in a saddened voice.

"Damn, they killed your seed? I'm sorry to hear that." Uncle Mikey shook his head.

"Facts, but I'm back now, and I'm back for blood, son. I ain't come here for that, though. What's good, you trying to make some big money?" YG asked, seeing his uncle's face light up.

"That's my middle name, money-making Michell (laugh)," Uncle Mikey stated.

"Check under your seat and just bring me back 30,000," YG said, seeing his uncle reach under his seat, pulling out a key of raw fishkill coke.

"Damn, my crystal dream." Uncle Mikey stared at the key as if it was a baby.

Uncle Mikey hadn't seen a whole bird since the 1980s, so this was a dream come true again. He normally sold 8 balls, or nickels and dimes for drug dealers, but he knew he was on now.

"That's you, just hit me when you done."

"Aight, son, I got you. I'ma go cook this shit right now." Uncle Mickey tucked it under his shirt and got out of the car, but he didn't see the gunman dressed in all black with a Draco to his side, creeping out the cut.

Tat . . .
Tat . . .
Tat . . .
Tat . . .
Tat . . .
Tat . . .
Tat . . .

Uncle Mikey's body got hit with the bullets as his body collapsed on the car. Then YG's car was sprayed with bullets while he pulled off, burning rubber out the lot.

Less dumped twenty-six rounds in the BMW, hoping one of the bullets hit YG as he raced off. Less was in Edenwald chilling when he saw YG parked up. He snuck to his car and got the Draco from his trunk.

***

Harlem, NY

G Balla was in Lincoln Pjs with two niggas, counting up money on money machines, smoking blunts of loud. G Balla was a Mackballa from Harlem who was getting money with his crew.
"Yo, G Balla, what's up with that red bitch from downstairs?" Fubu Mack stated, counting money.
"Shawty burning, bro, you don't want that bratty. That bitch catching bodies back to back," G Ball said, laughing, taking a sip of D'ussé.
BOOM!!!!!!
The front door was kicked in, and Fubu Mack picked up his 9mm handgun, shooting at the two gunmen.
Boc. . .
Boc . . .
Fubu Mack missed his target, and he received two bullets in the head for his effort.
G Balla and Third put their hands in the air, not trying to be another victim.
"Bag that bread up, ma," Lil' K told Red as he pulled off his mask.
When G Balla saw it was a young nigga, he couldn't believe he was getting jacked by a little nigga.
"Yo, little homie, you Blood? We da Macks. Why you set tripping?" G Balla stated while Red placed all the money in trash bags.
"Nigga, shut the fuck up!" Lil' K shouted as Red tossed the last stack of money in the bag.
"Yoo, son, Big Blazer gonna be mad. I owed him all that money," G Balla stated, making Lil' K and Red laugh.
"Nigga, a dead nigga debt is always paid," Lil' K said.
Bloc. . .
Bloc. . .
Bloc. . .
Bloc. . .

Bloc. . .

Lil' K killed both men as Red made her way down the staircase out the back exit where her brother and Blu were parked, waiting in the G-Wagon.

Bugatti Boy knew G Balla from years ago, and he knew he was moving weight in Harlem because niggas ran him outta the Bronx. G Balla was selling weight for Big Blazer on consignment, so Lil' K didn't just rob G Balla, but Big Blazer also.

Chapter 8

Long Island, NY

Fats was in his Hampton mansion worth $8.9 million, with seven bedrooms, four bathrooms, a six-car garage, full-court basketball, and a full court for tennis. The backyard was beautiful with a manicured lawn, gazebo with chairs, and a big L-shaped pool with a jacuzzi attached to it.

Fats saw Big Blazer walking his way towards the gazebo.

"Big man, what's up?" Fats had his own nickname for Big Blazer.

When Big Blazer came home, Fats blessed him with money, cars, bricks, and whatever he wanted, as long as he agreed to be on his team. Glock used to tell Fats about Big Blazer all the time, so since Glock was dead, Fats needed a replacement, and Big Blazer was the next man up.

"I'm great, fam, out here making this bag, son. I see you living like a boss," Big Blazer said, looking around before sitting down.

"It's all well deserved. Hard work always turns into success, but you have two types of success. One is overnight success, which is short lived. The second success is like an oven, something a good man named Ca$h used to tell me," Fats stated before taking a sip of water.

"That's a fact, OG, but we taking over the streets day by day. Success is an understatement for where I'm trying to go," Big Blazer said, cocky.

"Never get too big headed. Your head may explode," Fats said with a laugh, but was serious.

"When is the shit gonna be ready? I got everything in order for you," Big Blazer confirmed.

"Sometime this week everything will be in position, but what's up with Kazzy? His brother still locked up in VA, right now is the perfect time to get rid of Kazzy," Fats stated, wanting them dead.

"I'm on the hunt, don't worry about them. I'ma take care of them, they lightweight," Big Blazer told him.

"Don't sleep on them niggas. This is the same shit I told Glock, now look." Fats was honestly speaking.

"I'm not Glock," Big Blazer said before standing to leave.

***

Harlem, NY

Banger wanted to get out of the Bronx for a few hours, so he went to an after-hour lounge in Harlem. While he was in the lounge, he saw sexy Glenda in the hookah area with two of her girls.

Glenda was a thick, slim waist, pretty face, mixed chick with a nice set of eyes. She moved to Harlem last year and only fucked with ballers, but she always liked Banger, even though he was her brother Bugatti Boy's best friend.

One thing led to another and Banger had her bent over on all fours in the back of her Range.

"Uhmmm, shit, Banger, beat that pussy . . ." she moaned while he pushed deeper into her walls, gripping her waist.

Her pussy was so wet, he was sliding in and out of her. Banger felt bad for fucking his boy's sis, but she was worth the beef. He knew Bugatti didn't really fuck with her, but Banger always knew how to talk himself out a situation.

"I'm cumminggg, choke me!" she screamed.

Banger choked her, feeling her cream pour out. When she nutted, he was still horny, but she hopped off the dick and sucked him off until he shot a load down her throat. Banger was in love, but he knew this was all it could be.

"You got some good dick for a little nigga. I'm trying to see you again." She smiled, getting dressed.

"Maybe," Banger said, already dressed, sliding out the car.

***

South Bronx, BX

Red was leaving Michell Projects, walking across the street to her BMW. Today was a long day. The police arrested two of her workers and got two keys of coke. She hoped her workers kept it real and stuck to the code, but these days, niggas was snitching for nothing, so she didn't put nothing past nobody.

A van pulled up and hit the brakes behind her. Three gunmen hopped out with guns, surrounding her.

"Get the fuck in the van, bitch," one of the men said.

"Suck my dick!" she screamed.

Outta nowhere, two of the gunmen's heads were blown off with clean head shots. Red saw the perfect time to reach for her weapon.

Boc, Boc, Boc, Boc . . .

Red killed the last gunman. She saw Kazzy Loc walk across the street dressed in all black with a gun in hand.

"Even though me and my little brother don't see eye to eye, just look out for him out here. I see you got loyalty in your eyes," Kazzy said before walking off.

Red hopped in her car, dashing down the block, thinking how Kazzy just saved her life, but she knew he was still on the opposite side.

Romell Tukes

Chapter 9

Castle Hill Pjs, BX

Less was chilling in Castle Hill Projects early in the morning with his boy, No Balla, who had the projects on lock.

"Good looking on the come up, son. I got you in a week or two. You came through at the right time, family. My plug moved down south, so shit been brazy, boy. That's a fact. This shit gonna put me on the map, you heard," No Balla said with a book bag full of bricks on his back.

Less dropped off seven keys to No Balla so he could get right, because he knew he was a loyal nigga with a big grind.

"That shit ain't 'bout nothin', bro. I got you, son, but I gotta bounce," Less told him, looking at his phone to see Lady B, a bad ass stripper bitch from Brooklyn he'd been fucking with, calling him. He told her he was gonna take her shopping, and she ain't stopped calling his line since."

"Aight, bro, I'ma get at you, son," No Balla said before taking the drugs into his building.

Less walked through the middle of the projects to get to his car. Before he headed to Brooklyn, he had to slide out to MillBrook. Kazzy wanted to see him to check on him, but Kazzy also had a big lick set up in a few days, and he wanted to make sure Less was down.

Once he got in, ten undercover cop cars rushed him, almost hitting him. Less was ambushed by police with guns yelling for him to get down. Less refused and was tackled.

The police had to wrestle him to put cuffs on him, because he was going crazy biting police and everything. They found a gun in his possession, but that was nothing compared to what they were arresting him for.

Less was under arrest for the murder of Uncle Mikey in Edenwald Projects a few weeks back.

***

Sux2 Prison, VA

Knight was being escorted to E-Unit by three cops with his bags fresh out the SHU. Knight grew out his beard, and he had his dreads out, looking like a true Rasta.

"When you get your ass up in this unit, don't go stabbing up muthafuckers, tryna cut niggas' faces. All y'all New York niggas do that shit," a young CO dude told Knight as he walked into the unit, paying him no mind.

The first thing on Knight's mind was to get a knife and use the phone. Walking onto the unit, all the prisoners looked at him to see if he was from VA.

"Yo, bruh, where you from?" a fat nigga asked him, leaning on the wall.

"New York, why, what's shaking?" Knight said in his aggressive tone.

"Oh, you must be dude who be wilding. They call you Knight?" the fat dude asked, who was from Richmond, VA.

"Yeah, that's me, but it's some New York niggas in here?" Knight asked.

"It's two Brooklyn niggas, but they at rec outside, but what cell you going in?" the fat dude asked.

"I'm going to #147," Knight replied, looking at the paper.

"Oh, you going up there with Don, the homie from Bad News, good nigga. Come on, I'll take you up there," he told him.

"Don?" Knight stated, following the fat nigga, thinking why this nigga Don's name sounded familiar.

Once he went to cell 147, he saw the same dude who saved his life months ago when dudes attacked him in the cell with knives. Don was the one who stepped in and stabbed two dudes for Knight.

"Knight, what's up, bruh?" Don said, shaking his hand, remembering him from that rumble they had months ago.

Don was from Bad News, but he wasn't going to let them kill Knight, because he liked the way he moved and could tell he was a good nigga.

"I never got a chance to thank you for saving me that day, son, factz," Knight stated, walking into the cell.

"That shit ain't 'bout nothing, bruh, but you want the top bunk or bottom?" Don asked.

"It don't matter, you heard." Knight placed his shit on the top rack.

"I got everything you need hygiene, food, drugs, if that's what you into, whatever. All I ask is to kneel down when you piss dawg, that's all," Don asked.

"I take a knee to piss anyway, so that's nothing to worry about," Knight stated.

"Oh, here, take this," Don said, pulling out a long, sharp knife.

"Good looks, son, it's like you read my mind, bro," Knight said, tucking the knife in his boxers.

"I got plenty of those, but I heard about how you was putting on recently. Your name is litty in this joint," Don stated.

"Somewhat, I'm just trying to get home, bro. How long you got?" Knight asked, trying to get to know his new celly.

"I caught a gun, but my lawyer got me a low offer, so a couple of years," Don told him before showing him around the unit and to the two New York niggas who just came in from the yard.

Romell Tukes

Chapter 10

Manhattan, NY

BeBe was on her way home to her Bronx apartment from her job as a dental assistant. BeBe recently dropped outta college so she could focus on real life, but her main reason for leaving college was the death of her mom.

When her mother was killed, her whole life was flipped upside down. Knight was locked up in VA, Kazzy was deep in the streetz, and she didn't even see Lil' K anymore.

She felt like her once family was now broken into pieces. She had a strong feeling her mom's death was brought on by her brothers, but she didn't hate them for it.

BeBe just wanted her brothers back in her life, because they were all she had left besides her friends. She felt alone in this world, but she knew strength came from everything a person went through in life.

***

Soundview, Bronx

Lil' Blazer and a couple of his homies from his project just entered a basement party filled with strippers and hustlers. Since coming home, Lil' Blazer had been getting money and fucking the city's baddest bitches. Big Blazer was supplying him all the keys he needed and some.

Lil' Blazer even had his own section in the Bronx that was booming. He had YG on the team, so everything was going well.

Tonight was his little bro Gift's birthday, so he wanted to show him some love. Six strippers were in the middle of the floor having a squirt contest.

"I gotta fuck one of them bitches tonight," Gift told Lil' Blazer, who was throwing money. Gift was a cheap nigga, so he wasn't giving a bitch a dime.

"That's nothing, fam. You can fuck all them hoes if you want," Lil' Blazer said as one of the bitches squirted on his Balmain jeans.

***

"Let's just go up in there," Banger told Blu as they watched people walk in the back of the house towards the basement party.

"Nah, he gonna come out, just load up the Tech 9, cuz," Blu said, thinking about his brother, Black, who was a known rat, now hiding out somewhere. If Blu was to ever find Black, he would kill him by himself. That's how much he hated rats.

"That's him!" Banger shouted, taking him out his train of thought.

Both men hopped out when they saw Lil' Blazer and his brother leaving with two dancers.

Tat. . .

Tat. . .

Tat. . .

Tat. . .

Tat. . .

Banger hit Gift in his head with a straight bullet, and Blue hit another one of Lil' Blazer's homies. Lil' Blazer pulled out his gun while hiding behind the bitches as their bodies got hit with endless rounds.

Boc. . .

Boc. . .

Lil' Blazer shot Blu in his left arm as sirens could be heard, because a police station was around the corner. Banger and Blu got the fuck outta there before the police came and arrested seven people, but luckily, Lil' Blazer was long gone.

***

Miami, FL
Three Weeks Later

Kazzy was in Miami walking down South Beach Blvd on his way to a small ice cream shop. Paco came down with him, but he was on Collins Ave shopping, and Kazzy was here on business. Knight gave him a number and a name S, then told him to text that number and go meet his plug and he'd be good. Kazzy thanked him, because he was in need of a plug ASAP. Even though robbing was his number one hustle, it's just right he was focused on getting it the right way.

He walked inside the ice cream parlor and sat down near the window where no customers were at. Seconds later, a sexy red-bone chick pulled out the chair and took a seat while he was texting. When Kazzy saw how the chick was in front of him, he forgot what he came to Miami for.

"Excuse me, beautiful, but I'm waiting for somebody, if you don't mind," Kazzy said.

"It's cool," she said, not moving.

"They should be here any second," he replied, hoping she'd get the point.

"How do you like Miami, Kazzy? I'm sure this is your first time, because you the only nigga out here in timbs," she said laughing.

"How do you know my name, have we met?"

"I'm S, your brother's people, but my real name is Stephen," she said, seeing how shocked he looked. Kazzy never saw an attractive woman queenpin.

"Ok, so, I need like 200 for starters," he said.

"That's it?" she said seriously.

"Well, yeah, we just met, so I just want to make sure our business is good," he told her, looking around to make sure nobody could hear them.

While looking around, Kazzy saw all the bad Spanish bitches working in the shop on roller skates.

"I own this shop, so we can talk." She saw he looked a little nervous.

"I don't know nothing about you," he said, hoping this wasn't a set up.

"I'm from VA but moved to DC and took over the drug trade. I own a couple businesses out here in Miami, and I got a nice mansion in Miami Beach. I was fucking your brother. What else you want to know, how much I weigh? How many times I shit a day?" she said, annoyed.

"My bad... Ok, I'm down, whenever you ready, I'm ready."

"Good, Cash App me the number and I'll get with you." She stood to leave as her ass clapped in her loose dress.

"Damn, ma. . ." he said to himself. He couldn't believe Knight was fucking a bad bitch like that, and a plug.

Chapter 11

46th Precinct, Bronx

Sgt. Winstead was going over the caseload that had been on his desk for close to a year now, but he never paid it any mind until recently. Lately, every informant that came into his precinct had all been saying this Kazzy cat was responsible for all or most of the crimes that had been going on in the city. Looking back through some files, he found Kazzy and Knight being tied to close to a dozen murders last year.

Sgt. Winstead also got word that another crew of young savages was on the rise in the city. This was a big case, and he knew he had to take his time. He also had a lot going on outside of work in his personal life.

He just signed his divorced papers with his ex-wife after spending twenty-two years with her. His wife was a beautiful white woman who was a lawyer. His wife wasn't happy anymore, and she met a young man whose dick worked, unlike his. She was depressed, sexually frustrated, and overall not happy.

Sgt. Winstead was ten years older than her, a black man in his early 50s. He was husky, had gray hair, wasn't too handsome, but he had a good heart.

His son was twenty-five years old selling drugs in the streets. They didn't have a relationship, whatsoever, but he tried his best to see his son's children from time to time.

Sgt. Winstead had a bad drinking problem he tried to keep on the low, but a lot of people knew. His drinking was one reason why his wife left him.

He grabbed his phone so he could make his way to the local bar.

***

University Ave, BX

Ulissa was in the gym recording herself with her girl as they did exercise videos for fun and posted them up on social media. Ulissa was doing squats in tight leggings with small, ten-pound dumbbells, making the whole gym look at how phat her ass was and her phat camel-toe print.

"Damn, ma, you over here doing your thing. What's your name, cutie?" the muscle-head dude asked, trying to flex his pecs in his tank top.

"Excuse me, but I'm taken and I'm trying to record something and you're in our way," Ulissa said respectfully as the man didn't turn around, unaware her girl was trying to record their work-out session.

"My bad, ma, I'll see your sexy ass around, you heard," the man said, walking off.

"Hashtag, why niggas be so thirsty," her friend said on the camera phone.

They enjoyed the rest of the evening before going home to their men.

***

Two hours later

Ulissa and Kazzy were at the crib cooking dinner, talking about their day.

"Check this out, baby, I almost got over forty thousand views." She handed him her iPhone, showing him her gym video.

Kazzy stopped cooking to watch his girl's video, hearing a nigga try to holler at her. Kazzy saw some big nigga's back side.

"Don't worry about him, papi. He tried to holler at me, but you already know I curved that shit," Ulissa said, cutting up green peppers.

"I hear you in the background. That's my girl." Kazzy was about to pass her back her phone until he saw the big man's face. It was Big Blazer.

"Yeap," she said.

"Baby, what gym you go to anyway? I may sign up one day."
Kazzy handed her back her phone.

"I go to the one on University Ave. That will be cool, babe. We can exercise together." Ulissa was excited about this.

"I'ma think about it," Kazzy said, making other plans.

***

Rikers Island Jail
One Month Later

Less just got back from his speedy trial at court where he beat the murder charge, but the gun charge was sticking. He was happy to beat the man down. The gun charge was his least worry at the moment.

"Yoo. . .what's poppin', mack," his boy, Melly, from Cortlandt Projects said, approaching him.

"I beat that man down, son, it's litty, you heard," Less said to his homie.

"Yesss. . . I told you, bro. That shit was wild goofy, son. You had them beat," Melly said, walking with him to his cell.

"I'ma cop out to a two or three-year bid and go uptop. You already know how the macks moving up there, son," Less boasted.

"Factz, just be 050, gotta stay on point around them niggas. Shit be poppin' off. I just did five years in Auburn, shit brazy, Blood," Melly told him.

"I be knowing," Less said, about to go take a shower.

Romell Tukes

Chapter 12

Cortlandt Projects, BX

Bugatti Boy was outside having fun with a couple of niggas from his hood. He was only coming through to check on his workers in the projects. Bugatti Boy was doing good. He was finally getting money, and last week, he bought his first car, a BMW M4, all red.

Last night, his sister called him asking about Banger and to give her his number. When he pressed her about it, she told him they did some things and she wanted to see him again. Bugatti Boy was pissed. He was about to go to Mitchel Projects and punch Banger in his face, then whatever he wanted to do after that, Bugatti was down.

He felt like Banger violated the bro code by fucking his sister, and he cursed his sister out for having the nerve to call him and ask about his friend.

Bugatti's wifey was blowing up his phone, but he didn't feel like going back and forth with her, because he told her he was coming home an hour ago. His girl's pops was a big-time plug, but he hadn't even tried to get close to him yet because he had to think it out.

If he was to tell Lil' K, then her pops would be lunch meat for the crew, but he really loved his girl, so he had to plan this shit perfectly.

"I'ma pull up later, son," Bugatti Boy told some of his homies while walking off to his car up the block.

He was texting his girl when he heard the motorcycle roar down the block. Bugatti looked back to see if it was his older cousin, 5, on the bike, because he was the stunt man in the hood.

They didn't have on a helmet, so Bugatti saw his face, but he didn't see the gun he pulled out until it was too late.

Bloc . . .
Bloc . . .
Bloc . . .
Bloc . . .

Bugatti ducked and got his Glock17 out, shooting back hitting the bike, but he was missing his target as the bike took off down the street.

***

Bankroll waited until he got a few blocks away to slow down. Bankroll had been laying low watching Kazzy's crew and Lil' K's crew. He was focused on taking out both crews no matter what it took. He drove back home to his girlfriend to make love to her. He would come back out to the Bronx later to keep an eye on his ops.

Bankroll felt like he had the upper hand on his enemies, because nobody knew he was back for blood.

***

Lil' Italy, BX

Banger was inside a hole-in-the-wall strip club drinking and smoking blunts of loud as he got lap dances all night. Banger always went out when he got depressed or stressed. Since he was a kid, he'd suffered from mental health issues, and the only people who knew this were Red and Lil' K, nobody else.

The only way he could get over his troubled, saddened thoughts was to go out doing drugs and fucking bitches willing to give up some pussy. A cute, high-yellow, slim chick came up to him and started dancing on his lap, getting him aroused.

"Damn, daddy, that's how you feel?" the dancer said, liking what she was feeling.

"That's a fact," he said as she was popping her ass to the music, while he was blowing weed smoke in the air. "Pass me that drink," Banger told her, and she stopped and passed him a glass of Henny.

Banger gulped the rest of his drink, feeling it burn his chest.

"How about we finish this shit at my crib?" she said as he shook his head. The woman went to get her clothes and purse, in a rush, pulling out her phone texting someone.

Seconds later, she saw Banger looking fucked up. She grabbed his hand and guided him outside while on the phone talking to Lil' Blazer, who was a good friend of hers. She slipped a mickey inside of his drink when she was dancing. Banger was fucked up and he forgot who she was already.

The dancer was trying to force him into her Honda's passenger side so she could bring him to Lil' Blazer in Sandview to receive the $20,000 he had for her.

"Think you slick, bitch, let go of my fucking brother," Red said, pointing a gun to the back of her head.

"Please, he made me do it, Lil' Blazer. I got a son at home, please don't do this," she cried.

Bloc . . .

Bloc . . .

Red heard all she needed to hear as she put two holes in the back of her head. Red saw the whole thing since she slipped the pill in her brother's drink. Red was following him around because she knew how he got when he went through his depressed phases.

She placed him in her BMW and raced off before anyone saw her. Hearing the name Lil' Blazer was new to her ears. Big Blazer she knew of, but not Lil' Blazer, but she soon was going to find out.

Chapter 13

Highbridge, Bronx

Lil' K was parked outside of an apartment building in his new black Camaro SS, waiting on a cute chick he met days ago at a basketball tournament. Lil' K had been focused on getting money and locking down certain areas of the city. His crew was gaining more and more soldiers by the day.

His main thing was to make sure all his people eat by any means. Word was YG was back in Mott Haven Projects getting money, but he was letting a nigga named Bounty run the show for him.

A slim, cute, dark-skin chick opened the door and got inside.

"Hey, baby, I'm glad you came. Where we going?" she asked.

"City Island," he said, starting up the car as the *A Boogie Wit' da Hoodie* album came on. She reached for his Louis Vuitton belt buckle and pulled his dick out, smiling before she put her mouth on the tip.

Lil' K let her do her as he dashed through the city streets. He had tints on his windows, so nobody could see him. She was giving him some sloppy top, getting nasty on his dick as he stopped at the red light. Her head game was so good, his toes caught a horse cramp.

Before the light could turn green, he saw a nigga ice grilling his tints.

Tat . . .

Tat . . .

Tat . . .

Tat . . .

The man fired shots from a Mack 11 submachine gun, but the bullets did nothing to the car.

Lil' K pulled off, leaving Bankroll in his rearview mirror. Lil' K got his car bulletproofed the other day, because he knew he was about to be at war.

"Can you please drop me off? You could have got me killed," the girl said, shaken up from the gunshots that could have taken her head off if the windows weren't bulletproof.

Lil' K pulled over without saying a word, stuffing his penis back inside his pants, mad Bankroll just fucked his nut up. Lil' K didn't really know who the man was, but he was about to do his homework.

He dropped the woman off on the corner and made his way to Jackson Projects to speak to his young boy, YNG.

***

Yankee Stadium, BX

Lil' Blazer and two of his workers came out to watch the Yankees play against the Mets. This was Lil' Blazer's first time at the Yankee Stadium, and he lived in the Bronx his whole life. The place was packed shoulder to shoulder with people rocking their favorite team shirts and hats.

Lil' Blazer tried to send a little bitch from his hood at Banger, but his plan backfired, and now he knew his identity was exposed. Lil' K and his crew's names were ringing all over the city, and he wasn't feeling that shit at all.

"I'ma go get some snacks, son. I'll meet y'all over there," Lil' Blazer said, seeing snack stands near the bathrooms.

Lil' Blazer walked through the slow-moving crowd, unaware of the killers lurking behind them.

***

Red and Blu both wore Yankee hats and outfits, looking like a Yankee couple. Red had been on Lil' Blazer's ass for two days, and tonight, was going to strike her move in the perfect setting.

When she saw Lil' Blazer slide off, she followed him while Blu followed the two goons. Blu pulled out a long, sharp blade and stabbed both men in the side ten times apiece at the speed of light.

Both men dropped near gate 7 as civilians helped them, trying to look for the attacker, but he was gone.

Lil' Blazer was ordering some snacks when he saw a crowd rushing toward the exit, and he saw Red in the mirror above him with a knife out, trying to slide on him. Lil' Blazer pulled out his 9mm and started shooting at her.

Boc. . .
Boc. . .
Boc. . .
Boc. . .
Boc. . .

Red ducked, crawling under tables, weaving from his bullets as he tried to finish her. Red didn't bring her gun inside because she planned to use her blade on Lil' Blazer, but her plan backfired.

She saw Blu standing there as civilians were running all over the place at the sound of gunfire and two dead bodies near gate 7. Blu and Red got outta there just in time, because the NYPD was all over the place.

Romell Tukes

Chapter 14

Mott Haven, Projects, BX

Bounty turned the projects' playground into a drug strip. He had fiends going down slides before copping their fix. Bounty also started some shit called Crackheads Fight Club, where two fiends would fight for a hundred dollars of crack. The winner was the last man standing, and he got two hundred dollars' worth of drugs.

Tonight was a big fight with Big Cook, who won the last three fights. His opponent was a tall, skinny crackhead who used to box until the crack era hit the city.

Bounty was surrounded by his men as he watched the fiends square up and go blow for blow. Big Cook was throwing haymakers, but the other fiend swiftly ducked them. Bounty was cheering on Big Cook, who was from his build and showed him how to cook coke.

Bounty worked for YG, who was his cousin, but they never really had a solid relationship until recently when YG asked him to sell work for him at a 50/50 cut. Bounty just came home from upstate, so he was fucked up when YG approached him with the offer. While Bounty was uptop, YG's name was ringing heavy in the mountains for the work he was putting in.

"Knock that nigga out, son!" Bounty yelled to Big Cook, who was short of breath.

The tall, skinny crackhead took advantage of the moment and hit Big Cook with a three-piece combo, knocking him out.

"Damnnnnnn. . . Yoooooo!" the crowd yelled, seeing Big Cook drop face first into a sandbox.

Bounty turned around, and that's when he saw the gunfire, causing him to duck.

Tat . . .
Tat . . .
Tat . . .
Tat . . .
Tat . . .

Bounty got shot in his ribs while his little homies ran off on him, leaving Bounty to die. The two gunmen approached him bare-faced. It was Paco and a bitch, Hasley.

"Night, night, my G," Paco said.

"Sweet dreams," Hasley said before she put two bullets in his head.

Paco heard about Crackheads Fight Club ran by Bounty and knew tonight would be the best way to send YG a message.

***

Mount Vernon, NY

Chrishell was a beautiful Haitian woman with dark, smooth, beautiful skin, high cheekbones, good, long hair, and a nice body. If any nigga was to see her, they wouldn't have a clue she used to be a vicious coke and pill head.

She was Bankroll's wifey. They met in the same rehab center she now worked at five days a week. Bankroll changed her life. He was there for her when she needed someone in her corner.

Her family and friends all turned their backs on her when she was deep in her addiction. The only person who didn't turn on her was Bankroll, and that's why she loved him so much and planned to spend the rest of her life with him.

It was time for her to leave work, so she went to clock out and grab her things from the back. Chrishell knew how to deal with patients because she was once one of them, so it was very easy to understand and give her insight.

Walking outside to her truck, she didn't see the man with the hoodie a few steps behind her.

"Yo, ma!" the man shouted as Chrishell was about to turn around and tell him she wasn't no "Yo, ma."

When she turned around, all she saw was a chrome gun.

Bloc
Bloc
Bloc

Lil' K shot her in the face before jogging off down the dark street.

***

City Island, BX
Two Days Later

Bugatti Boy took Zendaya out to eat at Sammy's in City Island, which was a strip full of seafood restaurants.

"Why you not eating, ma?" Bugatti Boy asked her to see something was on her mind.

"My brother's girlfriend got killed in Mount Vernon, and I really liked her. She was good for my brother," she said.

"I never knew you had a brother," Bugatti Boy told her, because he'd never heard her say anything about a brother.

"Bankroll is my stepbrother," she said as Bugatti choked on his soda.

"Who?"

"Bankroll, he's from Sandview. I never told you about him because we didn't talk that much until recently," she said.

Lil' K was just telling him about a nigga named Bankroll they had to get rid of.

"Ok, baby, don't stress yourself. How about we go grab some drinks and head to the crib," Bugatti Boy told her as she smiled, knowing he was about to put that pipe game down.

Romell Tukes

Chapter 15

Downstate Prison, NY

Less was in A build watching TV in the prison they held inmates at before they shipped them off to their prison upstate somewhere. This morning, Less found out in a couple of days he would be going to Elmira maximum security prison.

Less took a three-year bid. He was trying to get two years, but the judge wasn't having that at all. He wanted to prove a point.

"Yo, blood, what's poppin'? They about to call chow, Mack," another prisoner stated, walking downstairs in his green uniform.

"Aight, bro, what's popping with that work-out, son?" Less asked. He'd been heavy on getting his weight up.

When his unit went to the yard, he did dips, pull-ups, squats, and push-ups with his homies. The Mackballers were deep in the prison where he was going, so Less knew he would have to put in some work and cut niggas in the face.

Less' unit was called to chow for dinner in the dining area where prisoners couldn't talk. The guards made prisoners walk through the tunnel in silence and in a line. If anybody was caught talking, then the big black cops would snatch them out of line and whip their asses.

Less couldn't wait to go to his prison soon. He was sick of downstate.

***

Bridgeport, CT

Dollar's wife was in the Korean nail salon getting her feet done. Ebony was a beautiful Indian and African-American woman with bronze skin, good, long hair, and nice facial features.

Ebony had a nice toned body because she stayed in the gym five days a week working on her body. She was a thirty-two-year-old accountant with a good head on her shoulders.

When she married Dollar, she had no clue he was suffering from PTSD or bad anxiety. He was having mental breakdowns, but she was there for him 100%.

It was a little late and she wanted to head home to prepare for work in the morning. That was her life. There were only two people in the nail parlor, her and the Korean woman doing her feet.

Dollar was in New York, so she had the house to herself, which was a blessing, and not only that, but she was having an affair with the garbage man. Her and Dollar's sex life had been on the rocks, and she had to get her rocks off someway.

The door opened and the Korean lady yelled closed, but the man walked inside, paying her no mind at all, staring at Ebony's sexy, pretty feet, making her smile. Ebony thought the man was really cute, but when she opened her mouth to say something, the man pulled out a gun.

Bloc. . .
Bloc. . .
Bloc. . .
Bloc. . .
Bloc. . .
Bloc. . .

Paco made sure both of the women were dead before leaving. He'd been waiting on her for over an hour, so he figured time was money and made his move.

Paco had a lot on his plate lately dealing with all his new ops, trying to stay on point, and doing his research on what he was up against.

***

Manhattan, NY

Fred was leaving a nice little club in the city, which was a suit and tie event, so he was dressed to the tee tonight. Fred was one of Big Blazer's workers, and he was also Sex, Money, Murder. Fred was moving weight uptown near Gunhill Projects, where he was from.

He and Big Blazer did a bid together back in the days in Greene State Prison, which they called gladiator school.

Walking across the street, he didn't even see the GMC truck coming his way.

BOOM . . .

The truck knocked Fred down, who was under five feet, so the powerful impact took him in the air before he came smashing down into the gravel.

"Ahhhh," Fred moaned, trying to move, but he felt like his back was broken.

A black pillowcase went over his little head, and two men tossed him in the GMC truck.

***

Forty-Five Minutes Later
Bronx, NY

Fred felt the truck come to a stop somewhere. He didn't hear his kidnappers talk the whole ride, which made him nervous.

At thirty years old, he never had these types of problems in the streets because he wasn't a gangsta. He was more so the getting money, hustler type nigga. He was also known to fuck a nigga's bitch.

The trunk popped and he was dragged on some rocks like a rag doll until he felt the pavement of some warehouse or garage.

"Y'all can take that shit off, son," a male voice said.

When the pillowcase came off Fred's face, he thought it was a joke, looking at a gang of Bebe's kids who looked his son's age.

"What's going on? Who sent y'all? Where y'all big homie?" Fred asked before Banger slapped him with his pistol, shutting him up.

"I want everything you have on Lil' and Big Blazer. I know you work for them, so save yourself," Lil' K said.

"Ahh, fuck, y'all them little niggas everybody been talking about." Fred cursed himself, because he always found himself in the mix of someone else's bullshit.

"You talk a lot," Red said with a chuckle.

"Big Blazer is on to y'all," Fred said.

"Fuck him," Bugatti Boy stated.

"Help us help you," Lil' K stated.

"I don't know where he lives now because he recently moved, but I do know his little brother got YG on his squad, and son is a hitter," Fred told them something that all of them already knew.

"Stop playing games wit' us. I'm tryna be patient," Red said, pulling out her gun.

Boc. . .

"Ahh, fuck, you crazy bitch!" Fred shouted in pain as she shot him in his left ankle.

"Talk, soft ass nigga," Banger stated.

"Ok, his mom lives on Morris Ave somewhere, and his pops lives on Crescent Ave," he cried in pain.

"Was that hard, goofy nigga?" Bugatti Boy pulled out his weapon.

Bloc. . .

Bloc. . .

Bloc. . .

Bloc. . .

Bloc. . .

Bloc. . .

Lil' K and Red aired Fred's chest out with rounds, leaving him there as they left the warehouse.

Chapter 16

Crescent Ave, BX

Mr. Moore was a vending machine fixer and a plumber for his night job. He was on his way home from a long day of work. Mr. Moore was Big Blazer and Lil' Blazer's father, but he disowned his kids years ago, especially after Big Blazer fucked his new wife outta hatred.

When he got divorced from their shady mother, he became a dead-beat father and disappeared. Both of his boys grew up hating him, so when he came back into their lives as grownups, they stunned him and treated him like a regular nigga.

His new wife and new life were amazing. Luckily, she couldn't have kids, so he was cool on that since he didn't want any more kids. He knew of his children's lifestyles, and he wanted to stay as far away from them as possible.

Once he got to his townhouse, he parked next to his wife's car and grabbed his work bag, leaving his licensed gun in the commercial van. Inside, he thought he was going to smell his wife's famous cooking, but he didn't hear or smell anything.

"Baby, where you at?" he yelled, taking off his boots, thirsty to get out of his dirty work clothes.

He went through the house looking for his wife, but he didn't see her. He walked into their master bedroom to see his wife tied up in zip ties on the floor, with two gunmen standing over her body.

"Mr. Moore, right on time, old head. We pulled on you because of your children. Can you give us any info? Your life and your wife's life may depend on it," Blu told him.

"I don't fuck with them hoodlums. They are no children of mine. Please, let us go," he stated, looking at his wife, who was crying, trying to breathe out her nose because her mouth was covered up.

"Mr. Moore, that's the best you can do for your wife?" Blu said while Banger placed his gun to his wife's head.

"Please, I swear to God, I don't know nothing about them sick fucks. I may not even be their pops, their mom was a fast one. She was selling pussy when I first met her, then I fell in love. . ." Mr. Moore admitted while his wife looked at him, never hearing this story before.

"You ready?" Blu looked at Banger, who nodded his head and shot Mr. Moore's wife in the head.

Blu then blew Mr. Moore's head off with his 357.

***

Clermont Park, BX
One Month Later

Kazzy Loc was in the park waiting for one of his clients to arrive from Harlem. Stephen was sending Kazzy so much work, he was overwhelmed. He was surprised how stern she was about her business. The product was great, and everybody was loving it.

Kazzy couldn't believe he was moving this much weight. He was scared somebody was going to jack him now, because he knew Karma was a motherfucker.

Normally, his crip homie from Harlem was always on time, but he was forty minutes late now. Kazzy hopped in his car, making his way out the park. On his way out, he saw a Lexus coupe parked in the middle of the road.

He saw it was his homie's car, so he hopped out to see if he was good. When Kazzy saw the man had four holes in his forehead, Kazzy pulled out his gun, looking behind him to see Dollar standing there with a big colt 45 pointed at his head.

"I've been waiting for this day. Y'all killed my brother, Glock, and my wife," Dollar said, looking at Kazzy with crazy eyes.

"Welcome to life, it's an eye for an eye in these streets," Kazzy Loc stated, showing no signs of fear.

"Eye for an eye. . ." Dollar was about to squeeze on the trigger until a cop car pulled up.

Kazzy saw Dollar distracted by the red and blue lights and slipped away, letting off two shots running backwards, but missing his target.

Dollar's worry was the police, because he just killed Kazzy's client, and going to prison wasn't on his agenda.

Bloc
Bloc
Bloc
Bloc
Bloc
Bloc
Bloc

Dollar hit the cop twice in his face before looking for Kazzy, who was now pulling off in his car. Dollar ran out of the park to his car parked across the street in a club parking lot. He knew he came so close to killing Kazzy, but he knew one day they would be able to finish what they started.

***

Michell Projects, BX

Lil' K, Red, Blu, and Bugatti Boy were in the back of the pjs talking about plans to get at Bankroll and to open up shop in Mount Vernon, which was only ten to fifteen minutes away. Lil' K's bro, Kritty, was a crip nigga from 3rd Ave, which was a big money strip. Everybody was sharing two bottles of Henny.

"Lil' K, I told you Kazzy saved my life a while back? I'm starting to think maybe you should put your pride to the side so we can get to a bigger bag," Red stated, seeing his face frown.

"That's a dubb, ma. I already told you that, Red. It won't work," Lil' K said, ending it.

"Yeah, bitch, get off Kazzy's dick," Bugatti Boy said, feeling the liquor. Red looked at him like he lost his mind and pulled out her blade. She stabbed Bugatti in his shoulder twice.

"Ahhhhhh, fucking bitch!" Bugatti yelled as blood poured down his shoulder staining his blue shirt he paid 1500 dollars for.

Red walked off with a smirk. She didn't take disrespect from anybody. Lil' K and Blu had to take him to MillBrook where an old lady, who was the hood doctor, gave him medical treatment.

Chapter 17

Uptown, BX

Lil' Blazer and a couple of his hitters were in the pool hall shooting pool, listening to a KJ Balla mixtape the DJ had on play.

"Rack them, son, how much you got on this game?" Lil' Blazer told his cousin, Tatto.

"Nigga, whatever, you put up, broke ass niggas!" Tatto shouted, making a couple of his goons laugh.

Both men put 10k on the table for good measure as they gambled ten stacks a game.

"I'm the one who got you your first pair of Balmain jeans, don't forget that, my boy," Lil' Blazer said before shooting the six striped ball in the corner packet.

Lil' Blazer had been all over the Bronx building his own empire separate from his brother. He always had his Blood Hound homies around him and a few Mackballers with him to hold him down.

Lil' Blazer was starting to move like a real boss. Even with beef, he was trying to focus on a bag. He was sending money and drugs upstate to his homies every week all over the prisons.

He and his guys were so focused on the pool game they ain't see the four masked gunmen enter the side door. The people that did see them made a quick dash for the other exit.

Tat. . .
Tat. . .
Tat. . .
Tat. . .
Tat. . .
Tat. . .
Tat. . .

Tatto's head blew off, leaving his brains on the pool table.

Lil' Blazer and his crew went back and forth with the shooters, but the gunmen had strong, powerful assault rifles tearing shit up. Lil' Blazer was crawling under tables trying to get away from the mayhem. A body just dropped in front of him, making him crawl faster.

***

Lil' K and his crew were standing there letting off their MP5s, hitting everything in eyesight. Lil' K saw Lil' Blazer make it to the door out the corner of his eye. He stopped firing and looked at his team, letting them know Lil' Blazer was gone and it was time to go.

They left four bodies behind them as they headed back to the South Bronx in joy. Bugatti Boy was the driver because he only had one good arm since Red stabbed him.

He'd been giving her the evil eye for a week now. He was ready to shoot her, but Lil' K told him he brought it upon himself. Bugatti knew how Red got down, so he knew Lil' K was right.

"Bugatti, can you drop me off at Michell?" Red asked from the back seat, but she got no answer.

Bugatti's face tightened as he continued to drive the truck, acting like he ain't hear her, making everybody in the truck laugh, even Red. They knew Bugatti really wanted to kill her.

***

Soundview Pjs, BX
Next Day
It was a nice day outside as Big Blazer walked out build 57. He spent the night at one of his side bitch's house, who could suck dick all night.

Big Blazer had to go to his father's funeral today, so he wanted to go home and get dressed. He didn't care for his father, but for someone to kill him was disrespectful to Big Blazer. He wanted his father's killers heads, and he knew there were only a handful of people who would have the balls to disrespect him.

When he spoke to Lil' Blazer about his dad's death, he laughed, danced and shouted that it was karma. Big Blazer also heard about his little brother's shootout at the pool hall, leaving Tatto, their cousin, dead.

Big Blazer was walking to his Audi and saw a bad little Dominican chick walking towards him.

"What's poppin', sexy?" Big Blazer said, stopping the woman, who turned her nose up at him.

"Ewwwwww," she said, looking at the booger hanging from his nose, and his breath smelled like shit.

"Bitch, fuck outta here, you ain't all dat." When Big Blazer picked his nose, he saw Paco hop out from behind a truck.

Bloc, Bloc, Bloc. . .

Big Blazer zig-zagged, seeing the Dominican chick shooting at him. Big Blazer pulled out his gun, firing at Paco and Hasley. A bullet hit Hasley in the shoulder as she was running back into one of the buildings, when the shooting stopped.

Paco helped Hasley to the car and made their way across town. He knew he shouldn't have let Hasley come back, but she begged him. He took her to the hospital.

Romell Tukes

Chapter 18

East Burnside, BX

Bugatti Boy just dropped his son off at his baby mother Karen's crib he recently got her so she didn't have to get on welfare like most bitches in the hood.

He met Karen last year at a block party in Hunts Point. The two kicked it off nice and started dating, then one thing led to another and Karen got pregnant with his son. The two had a rocky relationship. Since having a baby, they agreed to co-parent and only have booty calls once in a while.

"Bugatti, I told you I need money for clothes and diapers," Karen said, coming out the backroom from laying her tired son down.

Karen was a loud person, but she was beautiful, even after having a baby. She was short, light skin, and petite with a nice body. She used to be D Fatal Brim and Less' brother Kip Loc's wifey before he was killed in a nightclub by Glock.

When Kip Loc got murdered, she was devastated and hurt to the core, but she knew she had to move on. Once she met Bugatti, she fell in love, only to find out he wasn't who she thought he was.

Bugatti promised her he wouldn't cheat, and as soon as she got pregnant, he was fucking all her friends. He even fucked her sister in their bed and she caught them. That was the last straw for her.

"I left you $1,000 on the kitchen table," Bugatti told her, not trying to go back and forth with her.

He was walking to the door trying to get away from her.

"One more thing. I heard you was fucking with a bitch from 181st Street."

"What the fuck are you talking about, Karen?" Bugatti asked, seeing her put her hand on her hip.

"They call her Berry. She always wears that blue hair and she got a fake ass nigga. You know who she is. I went to school with her and she gave six niggas herpes," Karen stated seriously.

Bugatti knew who the chick was. She was in his car sucking his dick last week, but he refused to tell her that.

"I don't know who you talking about, Karen, and I use condoms on all y'all hoes," he said, walking out the apartment, seeing her little cute face turn beet red.

***

Sux2 Prison, VA

Knight just got called down for a visit, so he was in his cell getting ready. His celly was in the law library. Don was the coolest celly a nigga could have because he was laid back and chilled. Knight was glad he didn't have a drug addict as a celly, or a broke nigga, those were the worst.

While getting dressed, he wondered who was here to see him, because driving from New York to VA was a fourteen-hour ride. He left his unit on his way to the visiting room with his freshly done dreads he had touched up two days ago. Everybody thought Knight was from the south because he had a grill and dreads, but when he started talking, they knew he was a New York nigga.

***

Mita waited for Knight to come out. She thought he would love a surprise visit from her. She was looking sexy in a Chanel sunflower dress with sandals on her cute, manicured toes. A couple of visitors were there, but she was the center of attention, as always.

Mita moved back to New York where she was one of the youngest DAs in her firm, and the best. She had a thing for Knight. There was something about him that made her want more and more. Knight walked out, and she couldn't control her smiles. He was looking so good.

"Hey there, Mr. Bad Boy," she said as she stood up to hug him.

"You must like you some bad boys, and you smell good." He took a seat.

"Thanks, but how are you doing in this hole?"

"I'm ok, trying to maintain. It's some bullshit everyday in here," he told her.

"I just want you to stay outta trouble so you can come home. Do you plan on staying out here or coming back to New York?"

"I don't know yet."

"Oh. . . I think you should go back to New York," she added.

"Why?"

"Because you been in trouble out here and it could have cost you your life, so why go back?" she asked.

"That's the only reason why you think I should go to New York?" He smiled, trying to get the truth outta her.

"Yesss, well, maybe." She blushed, knowing what he was trying do, but she wasn't going to let him get it out of her today.

"I guess it's something for me to think about," he added.

"Please, I just want what's best for you." She was serious, because she knew he was a good dude.

"How's work?"

"Omg. . . the Bronx is wilding out. Every time I turn around, I see a new caseload on my desk. It's exhausting, you have no clue," she told him.

"That's the X for you, ma."

"I see bodies dropping left and right, especially in Soundview," she added.

Knight heard about a nigga named Big Blazer taking over the Soundview section, taking Glock's position. Knight switched up the conversation, talking about future plans, like where their first date was going to be.

Chapter 19

Williamsbridge, BX

Vena was on all fours, throwing her ass back on Big Blazer's dick. "Ohhhh, fuck, daddy, kill that pussy," Vena moaned, looking over her shoulder while Big Blazer went to work.

Big Blazer slapped her high-yellow ass so hard he left a red print on her right ass cheek. He started fucking her rough, like a crazy nigga fresh out a mental hospital. Big Blazer slipped his thumb in her asshole, and she quickly pushed him and his thumb outta her.

"Nigga, you bugging the fuck out!" she screamed on him because she didn't do the anal shit at all, and he knew why.

When she was younger, she was raped twice by two different men, and they both fucked her in the asshole.

"I'm sorry, ma. Come here, I got a little beside myself," he said, hugging her naked body then kissing her lips as she cried, because he knew better than anybody to violate her like that.

The two had been together on and off since they were kids, so they knew everything about each other. She was the only person who was holding Big Blazer down during his bid upstate, besides Glock. Vena was on visits, money, pics, and a 35-pound food package every month. She was a trooper.

She was thirty-one years old, sexy, and an ex-model and bottle girl. She was medium height, had colorful eyes, long, jet-black hair, which was fake, tattoos all over her body, and a big phat ass.

Vena was from Soundview Projects, so she was a hood bitch and a hustler. Big Blazer recently moved her into a nice area into a two-story house.

"I'm gonna take a shower. You're welcome to come," she said, ready to feel him down her throat.

Big Blazer loved being around Vena because he would forget about everything else. He had so many niggas at his head, he ain't know who was who. One thing he did know was Kazzy Loc and those new little niggas robbing his workers were on his Christmas list.

***

University Ave, BX

Today was a hot summer day, and the pool was packed with teens, kids, and adults trying to cool off that vicious summertime heat.

"I told you, bitch, we should have went to FDR Park. This shit is too fucking crowded," Briance yelled at her best friend, Christina.

Briance was seventeen years old and a dark-skin cutie. All the boys were always trying to holler at her, but she didn't want a man or sex partner yet. She wanted to wait until she got married. She was heavily in the church scene, but she still had a hard time with cursing.

"Let's go then. I don't want to be out here, anyway. Them niggas we met from Yonkers may be there again. If so, I'm fucking that tall, sexy one I was talking to. You can save that little bushy for Mr. Right, but this pussy for Mr. Right Now," Christina said, getting out of the pool to grab her bath towel.

"Whatever."

"You left your shit in the locker room, girl," Christina told her.

"Shit. . . ok, I'll meet you at the car."

Briance rushed to the locker in her little bikini, swaying her little ass. Inside, she opened up locker 47 and grabbed her phone and purse. When she closed the door, a man was standing there with a big steak knife.

She was so scared, she couldn't even move. The knife plunged into her chest and heart repeatedly, non-stop, until she took her last breath.

YG left her body there and slid out the back door of the shower room.

***

Mount Vernon, NY

Lil' K and Banger were in Mount Vernon with Kritty, a crip nigga from a block called 3rd and Union, where a bunch of crip niggas were getting money at. Last night, Lil' K and Blu hit a lick in Brooklyn for thirty keys, and they were giving Kritty five keys to get him started.

They had known Kritty since he was a kid when he was living in Mitchel Projects. He was wild but a loyal nigga to his bros.

"I'ma get this shit off in a couple of days, cuz, trust me. This shit be crackin' out cha son," Kritty said, sitting on two milk crates.

"I already know, say less, just get at us when you done and I'ma bless your game." Lil' K looked around the block to see niggas doing hand-to-hand sales everywhere.

"Aight, cuz, I been hearing y'all name heavy out here lately," Kritty stated, seeing one of his ops drive by. Kritty hopped off the crates in the middle of a conversation, shooting at the car in broad daylight. Lil' K and Banger got off the block.

Romell Tukes

Chapter 20

Lamburg Projects, BX

Sky was in her apartment grabbing diapers and bottles to put in her daughter's overnight bag. Sky was a cute Jamaican chick with a nice, small, toned body to fit her four-ten frame. Having a child by Blu was the worst thing she could have ever done, because he didn't do shit for his daughter. The only thing Blu did was come through to drop off money every week. They met in a strip club where she still worked.

In Sky's mind, Blu was going to be that nigga who was going to take her out the strip clubs and projects. But that wasn't the case at all. She was still on welfare in the projects and shaking her ass on poles.

Her daughter was crying, so she went to pick her up and rocked her with one arm while placing the bag over her shoulder. Tonight, her daughter was spending the night at Blu's house for the first time since she was born.

Leaving the crib, she took the stairs to see Lil' Blazer standing there looking like money in a diamond necklace and AP bust-down watch. Sky went to high school with Lil' Blazer and they used to fuck around, but what he was packing made her leave him alone. She knew why they called him Lil' Blazer.

"What's poppin', Sky?" Lil' Blazer asked, posted up as if he was waiting on someone.

"Hey, Lil' Blazer, I ain't seen you in a while. I heard you was locked up," she said, holding her daughter in place because she kept moving.

"Yeah, that's a fact, but what's up with you?" he asked, remembering how good her pussy was in high school.

"Now you know that little mini Twix can't fit up in this goodness," she said, stunning on him.

Lil' Blazer was so pissed, his jaw bone clenched, almost breaking. Lil' Blazer pulled out his gun, forcing it to her head.

"Yeah, bitch, talk that slick shit now. You ain't laughing no more, bitch." Lil' Blazer then placed the gun to the baby's head.

BOOM...

"Noooo!" she screamed. Sky ain't think he was gonna pull the trigger.

BOOM...

BOOM...

Lil' Blazer fired two shots into her head, seeing her body slump on the wall.

When he found out Sky was Blu's baby mother, he couldn't believe it. He wanted to ask her some questions first, but she crossed the line. Lil' Blazer had a little man complex because of his height and penis size.

He left the projects where his brother was on lock with the drug game. He was on his way to meet YG uptown near the RPT area.

***

Tremont Ave, BX

Paco was talking to his cousin, Sisco, about the money he owed Paco for three months now, over ten keys of coke. Paco hated putting family on, because they would be quicker to do you wrong than a person you didn't know from a can of paint.

"Paco, cuzzy, I got you. I just had to pay bills, my lawyer, and my child support, but give me a few weeks, and I got you," Sisco told Paco, standing in front of a corner store.

Sisco was a hustler, but he always fucked up a pack and he always got high off the work! He sold the ten keys within the first week he, but it took him three days to spend all the money, even Paco's cut.

"I'ma give you a month to get my shit, nigga." Paco was frustrated now.

Sisco looked down the street to see the person who he'd been waiting on. Last week, a man with no name paid Sisco 10k to meet

Paco in front of this corner store, and he took it because he knew Paco would come looking for his money.

"I'ma go grab some chips," Sisco said, trying to rush into the store.

"Nah, son, how much you got on you right now?" Paco said, making him stop. When Paco saw the crazy look in Sisco's eyes, he turned around to see Dollar about to hit him, but he ducked right on time.

Bloc . . .

Bloc . . .

Bloc . . .

Bloc . . .

The bullets hit Sisco instead of Paco, who was behind a car on the curb busting back. Dollar almost ran into one of Paco's bullets, but he was too well trained for that.

Then a man pulled up on a motorcycle behind him, shooting a Tech 9, causing him to dive on the floor. Dollar ran down an alley, ducking bullets from the Tech, running off. Lil' K made eye contact with Paco before racing off. Paco was pissed because he could have handled himself. He ain't need no little nigga's help, or so he thought.

Romell Tukes

Chapter 21

University Ave, BX

Big Blazer exercised in the gym, bench pressing four hundred and five pounds on his chest. Since he'd been home from jail, he stayed fit and in the gyms.

Business couldn't have been better for him. He was locking shit down, and now his little brother, Lil' Blazer, was doing big things. Last night, he and Lil' Blazer had a meeting about Kazzy's crew and Lil' K's crew. Both crews were becoming a problem, and they had to do something quick before shit fucked up his bag.

Big Blazer did two more sets and made his way to the pull-up bar and did ten sets of twenty real quick. People watched him work out since he came in the gym, and he was the type to show off when all eyes were on him.

The gym owner started to give him a job as a trainer, but he declined it because he didn't have time for that. He didn't even have time to really work out, but he forced himself to. It was time for him to go, so he went to get his gym bag and change out his exercise clothes.

***

Kazzy Loc stared out the windows of his car for Big Blazer to come out of the gym. He saw his car parked a couple of rows down, so he already knew he was here.

For a few weeks, he'd been plotting this since he saw Big Blazer on his wifey's exercise video in the background. He made Ulissa change her gym to a gym in Parkchester, and without questioning him, she did it.

Kazzy saw Big Blazer walking out the gym with a gym bag, looking drained. It was perfect timing for Kazzy as he slid out with his Glock 27 in his hand, ducking low beside cars.

***

Big Blazer was walking and texting his little side bitch, smiling reading her freaky message she texted him while he was exercising.

Bloc...

Bloc...

Bloc...

The shots hitting the car next to him put him on alert, making him duck for cover. For a big nigga, Big Blazer was swift at moving, light on his feet. Big Blazer left his gun in the car because he found no need to bring his weapon into the gym. Now, he regretted it.

Boc...

Boc...

He saw Kazzy's face as he tried to run down on him, but Big Blazer was finally at his car. Once in the car, Big Blazer pulled out the lot with his heart in his lap. He thought Kazzy almost hit him, but he was scratch free.

***

Kazzy saw he was gone and climbed in his car to go to PA because he had to go visit an old friend. He was upset that Big Blazer got away. He had to admit, Big Blazer moved nice for a big stocky nigga.

***

Waymort, PA
USP, Canaan

D Fatal Brim was in the shower after his morning exercise. Now he was ready to start his day. Since being in the feds, he'd learned a lot, especially about the federal law. He was so nice with the law, he was helping his homies get back in court.

He had a visit, so he was in a rush. This was his third visit since he'd been in the prison. Niggas would send him money and pics all day, but only few would visit, and a visit was like hitting the lotto in prison. The prison was always on lock down, so visits were rare for prisoners.

D Fatal Brim heard Less was upstate. He was upset about that, but he knew his brother was hard headed just like him. Since Kip Loc died, Less was the only brother he had left.

Getting out of the shower, he had his boots and knife on him. He was on some real prison time shit. Niggas knew how he was giving it up if something popped off. Inside his cell, he got dressed and went down to the visit room.

***

Kazzy embraced his boy before sitting down.

"You got your weight up, bro," Kazzy told him, seeing D Fatal Brim gained at least twenty pounds of muscle.

"I been focused on staying mentally and physically healthy, bro. I have no choice, or a nigga gonna be burnt out in here, son. Yo, you should see these niggas in here taking meds and drugs to fight their pain and time," he told Kazzy.

"Damn, I'm glad you holding your head up, bro. We miss you out there." Kazzy hated to see real standup niggas in his friend's situation.

"What's up with Black, he still ghost?"

"Yeah, we can't find him." Kazzy had been looking for Black's rat ass for months.

"When you do, bro, you know what to do." D Fatal Brim wished he could kill Black himself.

"Factz, but Less sends his love. I spoke to him last night," Kazzy stated.

"Tell him to get home in one piece, but what's popping in the town, crip?"

"Well, Lil' K got a crew of hitters moving how we used to, young and reckless. I tried to put him on some money, but he wants to get it out the mud. Lil' K saved Paco's ass, and the bro mad about that." Kazzy laughed.

"Damn, that's brazy."

"Yeah, they turning shit up, but I'm tryna see about Big Blazer, cuz in the way."

"When he come home? I hate that clown. I was uptop with him. He a bully."

"Son been came home, but fuck him," Kazzy said as they spent the rest of the visit talking about future plans, women, the past, and the crew.

Chapter 22

Brooklyn, NY

Banger and Blu were walking through the packed streets with two women they just met at JUVE, which was the West Indian Parade they had every year in Brooklyn.

"Yooo, you ready to bounce, son?" Blu shouted to Banger over the loud noise in the streets.

"It's whatever," Banger told him.

"Yeah, because we tryna fuck!" one of the women walking with them shouted. She and her friend were tipsy, half naked, and looking for a good time. They were already hot and sweaty from dancing through the Brooklyn streets.

Banger and Blu looked at each other, walking towards the train station to head back to the Bronx for a nightcap with the two freaks they just met.

This was Blu's first time coming out to JUVE, and it was worth it. Everybody wore paint on their faces, and the women had their ass and breasts out dancing in the streets, wearing their culture flags representing their islands.

***

YG was posted up on a building with four of his young gunnerz, drinking liquor and smoking blunts of loud. This was YG's first time outta the Bronx in months. He had to come out to Brooklyn for JUVE. It was the craziest event of the year.

"Pass the loud, Weezy. What the fuck you doing, fam?" YG snatched his blunt out of his homie's hand because he would smoke a nigga's shit up quick.

YG had been moving bricks in Mott Haven, Patterson Projects, and Uptown in the Bronx, but he was starting to get annoyed with Lil' K's crew, who was also trying to sell weight in one of his areas.

Smoking on the blunt, YG watched a couple of chicks twerk in the middle of the street. Looking to his far left, he saw Banger and Blu, the two niggas who he knew for a fact were down with Lil' K.

"Y'all strapped?" YG asked his crew, who all nodded their heads before following him up the street.

***

"Why are them dudes following us?" one of the women asked Banger, who turned around right on time to see YG lifting a weapon a few feet away.

"Duck Blu. . ." Banger shouted, getting low enough to dodge the first round of bullets while getting his pistol out.

Bloc. . .
Bloc. . .
Bloc. . .

Banger and Blu both shot through the crowd, hitting Weezy and another one of YG's hitters. Both of the women with Banger and Blu were laid on the floor bleeding from getting trapped in the crazy fire.

The crowd ran all over the place, making them lose YG, so they left, mixing in with the crowd rushing to the train station.

***

Manhattan, NY
Next Night

Kazzy was out with BeBe and one of her best friends, who was a bad little thick Puerto Rican chick named Molly. They all were out bowling, having a good time.

Shit had been so hacked, he didn't have time to spend with his little sister, and he hated that because family was everything to him.

"You strike out again," BeBe told him when he came to sit down after missing all of the pins.

"You not no better." Kazzy looked at his sister and her best friend.

"What's your name?" Kazzy asked BeBe's friend.

"Molly, I know yours already. BeBe talks about you all the time," Molly said.

"BeBe sure know how to run her big mouth." Kazzy evil eyed his sister.

"I'ma go get some drinks for you guys." BeBe went to go get them some drinks.

"So, where you from, Molly?" Kazzy asked.

"Well, I'm from Patterson Projects, but I live on White Plains Roads now with my boyfriend." Molly was proud to say she had a man.

"Ok, that's what's crackin'."

"How about you? I heard you got some model chick." Molly heard everything about him from BeBe.

"Yeah, something like that."

"Ok, me and my man, YG, about to go get my body done. I heard you got your girl's body done. How she look?"

Kazzy only heard the name YG, and he paused, blocking out whatever else she was talking about.

"YG?"

"Yeah, he from Mott Haven. You know him?" she asked with excitement.

"No."

"Oh, but I want to go to Puerto Rico. What you think?" she asked as BeBe came back with drinks.

Kazzy sat and listened to Molly talk about her and YG's relationship for two hours straight. Kazzy placed everything in his brain.

Romell Tukes

Chapter 23

Soundview, BX

Destiny drove to her mom's house to drop off her daughter to her mom for the weekend so she and Lil' Blazer could go out of town on a trip.

At twenty-five, Destiny had her own crib, car, and money. She worked for a Wall Street company downtown in the city. She was a beautiful sista with a nice, toned, curvy body. She stayed in the gym working on her squats.

Her mom was sitting on the porch when she arrived.

"Come help, Mom, you just gonna sit there?" Destiny yelled out her window.

Her mom was a heavyset, lazy woman who hated to babysit, but she did it from time to time.

"Girl, you been doing this shit five years now. Your fast ass needs help," her mom said, slowly walking down the stairs.

Destiny was getting her daughter's bags out the trunk, about to pass them to her mother. A motorcycle roaring down the block caught both of their attention because they were in a quiet, peaceful neighborhood and bikes were rare.

Destiny had the sleeping little girl in her arms.

The man on the bike had on a helmet, so his face couldn't be seen, but when he lifted a gun, their facial expressions turned sour.

Boc
Boc
Boc
Boc
Boc
Boc
Boc

The bullets hit everybody, even the little girl, who died before she had a chance to wake up.

***

Banger raced off on the bike. He thought Lil' Blazer would be with his baby mother because he saw him with Destiny for two nights straight. Banger wanted to send him a message to let Lil' Blazer know they were on his ass.

He shot across town and went to go meet up with Blu to talk about a lick he just came across in Westchester.

***

Peekskill, NY

Blu listened to his boy, Big L, talk for the last hour about this lick he was putting him on to. Big L told Blu about a kingpin nigga who lived in Peekskill, NY, upper Westchester, where he was moving keys.

Blu and Big L knew each other for years, but Big L went to college and had a family, so he left the street life alone and moved to Peekskill from the Bronx.

Earlier, Blu told Banger about this lick, and he told Blu that he would meet him in Peekskill.

"Yo, son, this nigga got over 100 keys in his spot," Big L said, driving his new Audi, speeding on the Bear Mountain Route.

"You said that about twenty times already, bro." Blu was starting to think Big L had a different agenda.

"I know, I'm just nervous. I never really robbed a nigga," Big L stated.

"Nigga, and you not today. I told you I'ma stake out the spot and me and my man gonna take care of it."

"I'ma still get my cut, right?" Big L looked at him, stopping at a red light.

"Yeah."

"Good." Big L didn't want to tell him how the nigga he was about to rob was fucking his baby mother and he wanted some get back. The nigga wasn't even close to a kingpin. Big L wanted to see him die, but he wasn't a killer, but he knew Blu was.

"How you know this nigga?"

"Who?" Big L played dumb, hitting 95 mph on a 75-mph speed limit.

"Who we about to rob?"

"My cousin told me about dude," Big L lied.

Big L sped by an 18 wheeler turning on a ramp and lost control of the car.

The Audi flipped over four times and landed on the other side of the road. Blu saw Big L was dead. Half of his body was cut off, out the window because he wore no seatbelt. Blu took off his seatbelt and climbed out the car.

There were three guns in the car, and Blu wasn't trying to be around when the police got there. He saw an exit a few feet away and limped into the small city and called Banger.

***

Soundview Projects, BX
Days Later

Lil' Blazer hadn't been himself since losing his baby mother and daughter. He tried his best to keep his family away from his lifestyle, but it caught up with him.

Lil' Blazer had a feeling it was Lil' K's crew because of the recent shootout in Brooklyn with YG and them. Lil' K's crew was coming harder than he imagined, and he was running outta ideas. Sitting in his car poppin' pills and drinking lean, a whole 8 oz, was the only thing taking the pain away at the moment.

Big Blazer just left him an hour ago, assuring him it was gonna be ok. He had some plans in motion, but he knew that wasn't gonna get his family back.

Chapter 24

Fordham Rd, BX

Window owned the auto body shop at the end of Fordham, which was a long strip full of shopping stores and regular stores.

Not only was Window the owner of the auto body shop, where people would come to get paint jobs, buy rims, tints, and car systems, but he was also the plug. His father was a big -time drug dealer in Dominican Republic. Window was from DR, but he'd been living in New York for ten years. He had a house in DR, a wife, and five children by two women.

The shop opened up normally at 8 a.m., but it was 7 a.m. now and he came in early, because last night his shipment came. Window had a routine where he would get his drugs sent to his front door. He had his drugs dropped off in his auto body shop in a commercial van with hidden stash spots.

Walking into the shop, he hit the lights in the front. Window's wide body had two red dots in the middle of his chest. His neck was so fat he couldn't even look down.

"Don't move, Big Pun, or I'ma punish your fat ass," Paco stated.

"How much?" Window already knew it was a stickup.

"No price, we already got what we came for," Kazzy stated.

Paco and Kazzy had been watching Window for over a month now, and they planned out everything to the tee.

They already had Hasley take the commercial van across town hours ago. They knew the drugs were in there because of how the Dominican men were acting so nervous on look-out.

Window looked around to see his van nowhere in sight.

"Shit," he mumbled, knowing they got him.

"Your shit gone, son, but you gotta charge it to the game," Paco said before firing three bullets in his head.

"Damn, bro, why you be so thirsty to kill a nigga? I feel like you be wanting all the shine," Kazzy said, leaving the shop.

"Nigga, you be all hesitating and shit, bro. I be having shit to do," Paco shot back, shaking his head, sliding his Desert Eagle in his back side.

***

Cortlandt Projects, BX

Bugatti Boy hated to lose money, and he just lost $7,000 on the *Call of Duty* game. He was past pissed off.

"Fuck this shit. I got better shit to do than sit here and play video games. That's broke nigga shit!" Bugatti shouted in front of everybody in the room, slamming the controller on the floor.

Bugatti Boy loved coming to his hood to chill with his young niggas. He had eight niggas selling work for him while he ran the streets robbing and killing.

"You just lost seven bands, bro. That's why you mad," somebody said.

"I'm glad you talking, little nigga. Where the fuck my five hundred dollars at?" Bugatti was heated now, and Lil' Mike owed him $500 for drugs he gave him to get on his feet.

"I ain't got it right now." As soon as Lil' Mike said that, Bugatti attacked him with his pistol, whipping him.

Bugatti Boy's homies had to get him off Lil' Mike, as blood was everywhere. Bugatti Boy left the crib in an uproar with three of his soldiers.

"Yo, you wildin'. That's the bro," Bugatti's cousin stated.

"Nigga, I should have killed that nigga, and he banned from the hood." Bugatti got off the elevator on the first floor and saw Lil' Blazer and three gunmen coming inside.

When both of them made eye contact, it was over.

Bloc
Bloc
Bloc
Bloc

Lil' Blazer hit Bugatti's cousin in his neck after one of his men dropped from an accurate headshot.

BOOM...

BOOM...

BOOM...

BOOM...

BOOM...

Bugatti's crew hit two more of Lil' Blazer's crew, leaving him alone.

Two police officers came up through the laundry as they were making their daily rounds.

"Put the guns down!" one of the cops yelled, before one of Bugatti's homies fired at one of the cops.

The other cop shot the shooter seven times while everybody else ran off, getting away from the police.

Romell Tukes

Chapter 25

Sotto, NY

Dollar brought his new girl to the fancy hotel he had for the day. Since losing his wife, he'd been lonely and horny. So when he met Cameron, he was wide open.

The little bit he did know about her, he was hooked, not only by her body but her beauty, and she was very smart. Cameron was a beautiful Latina woman who was a fashion designer for a big model agency.

He met Cameron at a gas station weeks ago and they clicked. The two had been building since their chemistry was beyond real.

"This is nice." Cameron drank wine out of a glass sitting next to him with her legs crossed, in a tight designer mini dress that had been catching his eye all night.

"You deserve the best." Dollar unbuttoned the top button on his collar shirt.

"I do, and that's why I'm here," she said, kissing his lips then climbing in his lap, undoing his belt buckle.

"Ummm. . ." She sucked on his lips, feeling his hard rod in her hand when she freed it.

Dollar lifted her dress up, realizing she had no panties on under. She slid him into her drenched love box, which was extra tight.

"Ugghhh," she moaned, grinding slowly on his dick, feeling him get deeper inside her.

She rode his dick until she reached her climax then took it out her pussy. Cameron saw his penis had her juices dripping from it, so she sucked him off, going crazy on his pole.

Dollar grabbed hold of the couch because she was about to make him cum. She stopped because she felt his build up. Cameron got on the floor in doggy-style position, and he got behind her phat ass, moving her ass cheeks out the way.

"Shit. . . fuck me, papi," she cried as Dollar buried his whole meat in her slowly, then he sped up while slapping her ass hard, turning her on.

Dollar was putting in work all night on Cameron until she had to leave.

***

Kazzy Loc was leaving Red Lobster, waiting on Ulissa to come out of the restroom. It was dark out and Kazzy was tired. He had a long day dealing with the new shipment that arrived last night.

Kazzy's business arrangement with Stephen was going good. She was strictly about her money, and he respected that. The bricks he got from Window, he put them up for a rainy day because he was flooded with work. Kazzy's main goal now was to kill all competition, literally.

A man with a hoodie and sunglasses on walked around the corner, walking behind him. Kazzy thought something was strange about the man, but he looked past it because niggas were weird these days, to him anyway.

Kazzy had his back to the man, texting Ulissa telling her to hurry up.

"I got you now, nigga," a voice behind him said with a gun pointed to the back off Kazzy's head. The gunmen took off his shades and hood.

"This part of the game, fam." Kazzy knew his day would come.

"Today's that day," Bankroll said, not paying attention to the red BMW pulling into the lot.

Kazzy saw a little chick creeping up on them out the corner of his left eye.

Bloc
Bloc
Bloc
Bloc

A bullet hit Bankroll in his arm, and he turned around, firing back into the darkness.

Kazzy dashed between two cars, getting to his gun, busting back making Bankroll take flight through the car lot.

"We even now, nigga," Red said, walking off back to her car. Red was with her friend, Andrea, going out to eat at Red Lobster when she saw Bankroll holding Kazzy at gunpoint. She felt as if she had to help because he helped her, and she knew who the gunman was—she saw his face.

"Babe, what happened?" Ulissa cried, coming out as she watched everything from the window with other civilians.

"Nothing, let's go." Kazzy left with her and spoke nothing of it again.

***

Sux2 Prison, VA

Knight was sitting in the dayroom watching TV while listening to his MP3 player. It was 8 a.m., so he normally watched the news then the *Maury Show* while eating oatmeal before his 11 a.m. exercise in the gym he did five days a week.

He couldn't wait until he was free. He was counting down the months, and he never wanted to come back to prison. He learned his lesson, but Knight had plans to get back in the dope game.

Romell Tukes

Chapter 26

Hunts Point, BX

Sgt. Winstead had been so focused on building a case on Kazzy and Lil' K, who he found out were brothers and responsible for most of the city's murders.

He got a call from one of his special informants saying they had some reliable info for him to help his case out. Sgt. Winstead arrived behind an old factory where drag racers came to race every weekend for car meets.

There was a blue Honda, and his snitch, Wing, hopped out the driver seat to greet him. Wing's name used to be heavy in the South Bronx. He used to be a shooter until he got jammed for a body and started telling on niggas.

Since then, Wing had been working for the police, and he had no remorse. Wing even got his blood brother 60 years in state prison.

"What you got for me, Wing? Tell me something good, gangsta." Sgt. Winstead was excited because this could be the big break he needed.

"I'm sorry man, I have to." Wing's awkward look made Sgt. Winstead feel uneasy.

Wing pulled out a gun and pointed it at Sgt. Winstead's face. The passenger door to the Honda opened, and Lil' K stepped out with a Mack 10 in hand.

"Some people don't know how to mind their own fucking business. That's the problem with people nowadays," Lil' K stated while staring at Sgt. Winstead's upset face.

"You kill me, I swear they will bury you and your fucking crew under the jail," Sgt. Winstead spat, looking at Wing in disgust.

Banger and Blu had Wing's mom, sister, and son all tied up at their house, as ransom for Sgt. Winstead. Everybody in the Bronx knew Wing was a big rat, and he was Blu's cousin. He told Blu that

Sgt. Winstead was building a big case on them and Kazzy, so they had to do something.

Lil' K aimed his gun at Wing, who had his gun on Sgt. Winstead, sticking to the game plan.

Tat. . .

Tat. . .

Tat. . .

Tat. . .

Wing's body dropped after the hollow tip ripped through his brains. Sgt. Winstead looked at Wing, and he started to beg for his life until Lil' K shut him up.

Lil' K left both men's lifeless bodies there and walked off to the car he had Wing steal.

***

Queens, NY

Big Blazer's friend had a big album release party in Club Angle, and the place was packed tonight. Big Blazer and three of his goons were leaving the club, on their way to the afterparty in Manhattan.

"Yo, that shit was poppin', blood," one of his goons said.

"Nigga, that shit was trash, B. I ain't never going back in there. Them bitches all look dirty," another one of Big Blazer's goons shouted, walking out the club.

***

Banger and Bugatti saw Big Blazer and his crew walking out the club and jumped out the truck, trying to be low. They knew Big Blazer was coming out to this album release party because word was, Big Blazer was the one who put the money behind the rap artist to get him started.

"Don't fuck this up," Banger told him.

"Nigga, shut up, and that's fucked up how you fucked my sister." Bugatti had been holding this conversation for a while.

"What?"

"Nigga, you know what I'm talking about. I should fuck your sister so you can see how I feel," Bugatti stated, striking a nerve.

"You know Red don't like niggas, but can we talk about this later." Banger saw Big Blazer crossing the street.

"I should shoot your dumb ass by mistake, goofy nigga," Bugatti mumbled, ready to put in work.

***

Paco was in his Acura watching Big Blazer and Banger and Bugatti Boy. He came here to get Big Blazer, but he didn't see Lil' K's crew until seconds ago.

Paco wasn't going to let no little niggas outdo him or show him off, so he hopped out with a big .45 pistol. When he got out, shots started to ring out between Big Blazer and Banger.

Boc. . .

Boc. . .

Paco hit one of Big Blazer's goons, taking them by surprise. Banger and Bugatti looked at Paco, pissed off, ready to shoot him, but they were too busy ducking bullets.

BOOM. . .

BOOM. . .

Paco shot Big Blazer in his legs as twenty niggas came out the club to help Big Blazer.

Bloc . . .

Bloc . . .

Bloc . . .

Bloc . . .

Bloc . . .

Banger and Bugatti looked at Paco, who was shooting at the group of niggas shooting at them. When Paco ran outta shells, he climbed back in his car, racing off.

Banger and Bugatti did the same thing as a hail of bullets came down on them like a rain shower. Banger, Bugatti, and Paco all made it out alive.

Chapter 27

Connecticut

Dollar was leaving his home going to handle a very important mission. He was going to see Red's father, who was a veteran. Dollar knew Red and Banger's father. He was with him in the army until he started going crazy.

He got word from one of his fellow soldiers that their father was in a VA shelter in the Bronx. One thing Dollar was good at was playing dress up, and today he was dressed up as a doctor to get in the VA shelter, which was built like a hospital.

While he was driving, he was thinking about his new girlfriend, who he was head over heels for, Cameron. She was all he'd been thinking about for days. She reminded him so much of his recent wife. The chemistry was strong, but he wanted it to be a little stronger.

***

Hour Later
Burnside, BX

Dollar pulled up to Harris Ave and parked on the corner in front of the nursing home. He got out with a briefcase and white lab coat, wearing glasses, looking like a true doctor.

Once inside, the place was clean. The floors were so shiny he could see himself in the reflection. Luckily, he saw nobody at the front desk, so he took it upon himself to look in the log book for Jerry's room number.

When he saw Jerry was in room 114, he walked down the hall, passing vets in wheelchairs dazed into the walls. Dollar was happy he wasn't too far gone from being in the war, but he also knew he wasn't as mentally stable as he should be.

Walking down the long narrow hallway, he realized room 114 was at the end. Dollar brought a blade with him under his peacoat beside a gun, which would alert everybody.

Dollar opened the room door slowly and saw Jerry climbing in a chair as if he couldn't walk. Jerry was paralyzed from the waist down from an attack that happened on his last tour.

"Jerry?"

"Yeah, who are you?" Jerry looked at Dollar, never seeing him before in the hospital because he knew all the pretty, young female doctors. He tried to grab all of their pussies at least once a day.

"I'm a long-time friend." Dollar closed the door and took off his glasses. When Jerry saw who it was, his heart stopped for a second.

"Help!" Jerry screamed one time, but it was pointless because Dollar was already plunging the knife in and out of him until Jerry's body got still, unable to move.

Dollar saw his job was done and left the hospital.

***

Miami, FL

YG and Lil' Blazer were in Miami having the time of their lives. Lil' Blazer rented an A&P mansion in Miami Beach for the week just to get away from everything going on in New York.

They were throwing a big pool party and a lot of females came out. They had an outside bar and kitchen, so the crowd was having the best time of their life.

"Yo, this shit the wave, son," YG said with a water gun in his hand.

Bitches were on the jacuzzi twerking for the crowd, having a contest for the best twerker.

"We had to get away from the city, bro. I'm upset Big Blazer ain't come, bro." Lil' Blazer sprayed two women with his water gun as they ran around in bikinis.

The two partied all night and had a good time in the club, where they met YFN Lucci after he performed.

***

Michell Projects, BX
Two Weeks Later

Red and Banger were at their father's funeral, looking around to see nobody there. When their mom told them about their father's death, Red didn't give a fuck. She disliked him anyway, but Banger explained to her that to move on in life, you had to forgive people.

They both knew his death was because of them. Somebody after them went to their father and stabbed him to death. Little did the killer know, they had no connection with Jerry at all. They had changed up the way they moved now, because it was war time.

Lil' K had plans to take everybody to Abu Dhabi in a few days.

Romell Tukes

Chapter 28

City Island Seafood, BX

Kazzy leaned back in his car while Molly was sucking his dick at a fast speed and slurping on his precum at the same time.

"I love your dick," she told him as she went deep down, her throat burying his pole down the back of her mouth.

Molly got Kazzy's number from BeBe a few days ago when YG went to Miami with Lil' Blazer. She found out YG was cheating before he left and he got some bitch pregnant, which crushed her heart.

Molly had a crush on Kazzy ever since she saw him, but she was heavy on loyalty, and cheating on YG was out the window, until she caught him cheating. When she called Kazzy, she asked him if he wanted to go out to eat at City Island, and he agreed.

Once they ate and talked, Molly wanted to fuck so bad, but her period came on yesterday, but she loved sucking dick. She wasted no time in sucking dick, and Kazzy was loving it.

"Ummmm . . ." he moaned.

Molly felt him shoot a load down her throat, and she swallowed it, wiping his dick clean with her tongue.

"How you like that? I bet your girl can't suck dick like that."

"Nah." Kazzy fixed himself up and started the car, pulling off.

"It was nice chilling here with you today. I needed this, Kazzy."

"Yeah, me too. You a cool little chick, just don't tell BeBe about this," Kazzy repeated.

"I was going to tell you the same thing," she replied, knowing how BeBe was over her brothers.

"Bet."

"Can I tell you something?"

"Sure." Kazzy jumped on the highway to take her home to the Castle Hill area of the Bronx.

"I know about your beef with YG and his friends." She was nonchalant.

"I don't know what you mean."

"Yes, you do. I may look dumb, but I'm not. I've heard of you before I knew you were BeBe's brother."

"So, you saying all this to say what? You gonna tell him?" he asked.

"Never, I want to help you, if you let me. I'm cutting that nigga off," she told him, staring in his eyes, ready to give him her love.

***

Abu Dhabi, United Arab Emirates

Lil' K, Red, Banger, Blu, and Bugatti Boy and his girl, Zendaya, all got off the flight in Abu Dhabi.

"Never bring sand to the beach," Lil' K told Bugatti Boy in a low-pitch voice as they walked through the airport.

"Nigga, mind your business. If wifey wanna come, then that's on her," Bugatti Boy shot back, catching up with Zendaya.

"Yo, KeKe." Red always called Lil' K KeKe.

"What's good?" Lil' K slowed down, taking her heavy bag for her. "Damn, what you brought the gun store with you, my nigga?" Lil' K played.

"Shut up, but I'm not tryna share a room with Banger. He gonna have wild bitches in there. I know his nasty ass, so let me share a room with you? The hotel outta rooms," she stated.

"Aight, it's one bed. I got the left side, and you better not snore." He knew she didn't snore because they slept in the same bed many times.

"Got you." She climbed in the big van on their way to the ho-tel/resort.

***

Hours Later

Lil' K, Banger, and Blu were in the outdoor pool area drinking with six bad ass Arabian women, trying to fuck.

Lil' K was happy to see his boys tripping out, having fun. He was in the corner of the pool alone, sipping on white Henny.

Bugatti Boy was upstairs fucking his girlfriend, having the time of his life, because she wasn't letting him come outside around no hoes.

Red walked out in a silk robe , and when she dropped her robe, Lil' K was beyond shocked seeing her sexy body in a bikini two-piece. Lil' K's dick was so hard he tried to look elsewhere, but Red was coming his way.

"Thanks for sharing the room wit' me bestie." She hugged him, feeling his pole press against her coochie, making her jump back. Looking down at him, she saw how embarrassed he was and started talking about the stars in the sky.

Lil' K and Red drank the white Henny together and talked for two hours. Banger and Blu left with the women.

"Can I tell something? And promise you won't judge me or look at me less," she stated.

"I won't."

"I want you to fuck right here," Red said in her innocent voice as she stood in front of him, between his legs.

"What, are you sure? Red, you drunk."

"No, I'm not. I've been dreaming about this since we were kids," she admitted, rubbing on his hard manhood.

Lil' K always thought she was gay because he knew she had a girl once, but he stayed outta her love life.

"I always wanted you too." His words shocked her heart. She kissed his lips softly.

He placed her on the wall and moved her bikini panties to the side and lifted her in the air. His pole slowly eased into her tight-ness.

"Ugghh . . ." she cried, feeling him open her pussy walls. Lil' K slowly worked his way into her, making her go crazy.

"Damn, your pussy good. I love you," he cried, going deeper into the best pussy he ever had.

"I love you too. Oh my god, I'm cumming," she screamed as he continued to fuck her until she climaxed into the water.

Lil' K bent her over, and she grabbed the edge of the pool while Lil' K fucked the shit outta her, making her scream throughout the whole resort, waking people up.

Chapter 29

Elmira State Prison, NY

Less walked out the mess hall, on his way back to the unit with a group of Bloods, mainly Mackballers.

Being in an environment like Elmira, which was a maximum security prison in upstate New York, a nigga had to stay on point. A nigga was getting stabbed or cut in his face every day. Less knew a lot of niggas from the Bronx and a lot of dudes heard of him.

Less spent his days walking the yard and exercising, lifting weights five days a week. His crew, Kazzy Loc and Paco, still kept in touch with him, giving him money and so forth.

Everybody heard of Kazzy Loc and Knight. Even though Kazzy was a crip and the state prisons were filled with Bloods. Kazzy Loc's name was respected, and he never even touched a prison yard.

"Yo, son, you going down for a visit this weekend?" East Balla asked Less.

"Nigga, you know I'm going down for a visit," Less replied, because every Friday, he asked him the same shit.

"Can your people pick up my girl, bro?" East Balla's girl drove up with Less' girl every weekend.

"My girl pick up your girl every weekend, right?" Less hated dumb questions.

"I just wanted to make sure."

Less walked in his unit on the second level, going to his cell to take a nap because he had a long day.

***

Burnside

Paco sat in the SUV listening to a Ty Dollar Sign's album, watching the main entrance of the Bronx Community College. Paco was waiting on Bankroll's sister to come out since he saw her go inside two hours ago.

Bankroll was back and Paco had some unfinished business with him, and he couldn't wait to kill him, but until then, he had plans to get his sister.

***

Zendaya checked her watch, walking through her school, B.C.C. It was 6 p.m. and she had plans to go out on a dinner date with Bugatti Boy.

Since coming back from Abu Dhabi, she'd been meaning to have a sit down with Bugatti, but he'd been running around too much. Today, she felt it was the perfect time to tell him she was leaving him for a nigga she recently met on Fordham Road.

She was leaving him for a sexy, dark-skin nigga who just came home from federal prison. Bugatti was doing too much. She knew he was cheating, and she was doing the same thing. She wanted to tell him before their trip, but Zendaya always wanted to go on a vacation to Abu Dhabi.

Walking out of her school, she headed to her car parked across the street. Once she threw her books in the back seat of her car, when she closed her car door, a man was standing there.

"Hey, can I help you, god damn?" Zendaya shook her head.

Paco grabbed her by her small neck and choked her with one hand, then Paco pulled out his gun with the other hand, pressing it to her head.

"Tell me where I can find Bankroll."

"Mount Vernon."

"Where, bitch?" Paco needed accurate information on Bankroll.

"I really don't know, please," she cried.

Bloc
Bloc
Bloc
Bloc

124

Paco shot her in her face multiple times, seeing her body drop, and walked off. He had to go meet Hasley, who was waiting for him in the Heights.

***

Paco pulled into the BP gas station to see a black Range parked near the restroom area. Paco was pressed for time because he had to go check Kazzy to talk about YG. He had some info on him.

"Hasley, what's up, baby?" Paco climbed in the truck, kissing her soft lips, seeing her mood was off.

"Hey."

"What's wrong, baby?" Paco asked.

"I'm pregnant." Hasley's words hit him like a knife.

"Ok, when you going to get the abortion?" he said flatly, seeing tears quickly fall down her face.

"Get the fuck out!" she yelled, hurt by his words.

"Hasley, we not ready for a baby, you know that." Paco tried to clean up his response.

"Please, get out. . ." She wiped her tears as he got out, upset. Paco knew having a child right now was bad timing.

Romell Tukes

Chapter 30

Williamsbridge, BX

Vena pulled up into her driveway, turning off her car, glad Big Blazer wasn't there at the moment. Whenever his truck was gone, so was he, and right now she didn't even want to look at his face. Yesterday, Vena caught Big Blazer fucking some hoodrat bitch inside his truck in the back of Soundview Projects. Vena's cousin lived in the building, so she was there visiting her. On her way out the build, she saw Big Blazer's windows fogged up and his car was rocking.

Looking deep into the tints, she saw him fucking her cousin's daughter. Vena went crazy and ended up beating up her cousin's daughter and Big Blazer, and she got arrested because the police saw it all.

Luckily, Big Blazer bailed her out that same night, but Vena was done with him. She was there to pick up some clothes and get her shit to go stay at her aunt's house.

Vena walked in the crib, closing the door behind her and turning on the light in her living room to see a man pointing a gun at her.

"Ohhh my god!" she shouted.

"Shhhh . . . " Kazzy Loc told her to sit down on the couch.

"He doesn't keep money here. He keeps shit at his cousin's crib in Soundview." She already knew what he wanted, so there was no use for her to play games, she thought to herself.

"Is he coming here?" Kazzy had been waiting in Big Blazer's crib for hours, and he was just about to leave. He searched the whole crib for money and drugs already and found nothing, so he knew Vena was telling the truth.

"No."

"Where can I find him?"

"He's all over the place, but normally he's with his cousin, 45. They got the stash house on Smith Street in Soundview on the same block as the corner store and Crown Fried Chicken," she stated.

Kazzy Loc heard all he needed to know.

Boc...

Boc...

Boc...

Boc...

Boc...

Vena's body was still moving after the five shots to the chest.

Boc...

The last bullet crushed into her brain, killing her for good.

Kazzy left her crib, calling Paco, telling him about 45.

***

Forty-Five Minutes Later

Big Blazer saw Vena's car parked in front of their home. He knew had some explaining to do, and he was about to kiss her ass. He jumped out with some roses, walking into the house.

"No, no, no, no..." Big Blazer dropped the flowers, panicking, shocked to see his lover dead on the couch.

Big Blazer had tears in his eyes. He couldn't stand there and look at her any longer.

***

JFK Airport, Queens

Lil' Blazer and YG's flight landed in New York at 8:15 p.m. Both men were drained, sleepy, and had jet lag.

"That was a good trip. We needed that, you heard," YG stated, walking through the airport.

"Factz, son, you was turned up, but I think one of them bitches burnt me. I been pissing funny all day," Lil' Blazer said, scratching his dick.

"That's why I don't be fucking after niggas," YG joked.

128

Lil' Blazer had two of his goons waiting for him in the lot with guns for them. As soon as they landed, Lil' Blazer was back on war mode.

Big Blazer texted him yesterday telling him about Vena's death and how he was going outta town for a while, and he wanted him, 45, and the gang to hold shit down.

Walking through the lot side by side, they never saw the man creeping up behind them.

BOOM...

BOOM...

The shots put both men on alert, causing them to duck and run, rushing to the GMC truck.

BOOM

BOOM

Paco was chasing them through the lot. Paco already killed the two shooters in the GMC with his silencer attached to his gun.

Lil' Blazer and YG made it to the truck, moving the two bodies out to the ground before climbing in the truck. YG caught a bullet to the upper back as he yelled in pain.

The GMC truck pulled off while Paco continued to shoot, emptying his clip.

Chapter 31

Uptown, Bronx

Marlyn had a gambling spot near Boston Road, which he'd been running for years. He was a full-blooded Jamaican from Kingston. His family had a heavy name in the streets of Jamaica.

In the basement of a building he owned, he used to run his gambling spot, which made close $50,000 a day. Marlyn charged niggas for gambling fees and house taxes. Marlyn also ran a big molly drug operation that he was making millions off of.

His Atlanta plug always looked out for him and blessed him with tons of molly by the shipment.

"Damn, bloodclot, mon!" Marlyn yelled, losing the poker game.

"Yesss!" Marlyn's friend, JaJa, shouted, winning $15,000 in poker chips.

BOOM!!!! The basement door flew open as two men bust inside.

Boom. . .

Boom. . .

Boom. . .

The shotgun blast from Paco put three big holes in JaJa's chest because he tried to move.

"Waittt!" Marlyn screamed with his hands in the air.

"Nigga, fuck all that, where the money?" Kazzy Loc shouted, watching the other Rasta in the corner.

"I have money under the bar counter, take it all, please," Marlyn said with a sad look.

Paco went to check the bar as Kazzy saw the other Jamaican reaching for a gun.

BOOM. . .

BOOM. . .

The man's head flew off his shoulders. When Marlyn saw that, his eyes widened, almost making his eyes pop out. Kazzy Loc now had his weapon trained on Marlyn, who was scared to move.

"Yo, this is it, we good, you heard, bro!" Paco shouted with a big trash bag full of money in his hand.

"So, we crisp, brother?" Marlyn's voice was shaky.

"Yeah, we good" Kazzy fired one bullet that took off half of Marlyn's face.

"You driving, bro? That gun blast got my fucking wrist hurting, cuz," Kazzy told Paco, leaving up the stairs that led into the back of some rundown apartment builds.

"We gonna handle son right now or you want to wait?" Paco placed the bag in the backseat of their car.

"Let's get this shit over with, plus, it's 2 a.m. Saturday. It's the perfect time to catch him," Kazzy stated, climbing in the passenger seat.

***

Minutes Later
Soundview, BX

Paco parked across the street from a two-story house, which belonged to 45, who was Big Blazer's cousin and worker.

"That's it, but nobody is home, bro. I told you we should have came another day." Paco was running outta patience. Lately, he'd been upset and stressed due to Hasley's pregnancy.

"Nigga, calm down, bro. That bitch been having you go crazy, son," Kazzy told him, seeing HD lights on a car coming their way.

"Here he go." Paco ignored Kazzy's statement, pulling out his gun.

***

45 pulled into his parking spot ready to hit the sack and get some sleep. He was tired from clubbing with Head and Holiday.

He was moving bricks for Big Blazer, and he kept a stash house inside his crib, but he was outta drugs. Tomorrow, he had plans to go drop off the $400,000 he had in his crib for their re-up.

Climbing out his Porsche, he was a little tipsy off Henny and Remy Martin he was drinking in the club with his crew. When he closed his car door, two gunmen approached him, grabbing his shirt collar. 45 was a small dude, so it was easy to yank him up.

Paco took the Glock 45 from the man's waistline.

"Take us inside, and no funny shit, you heard," Paco whispered into 45's ears.

45 took both men into the polished crib, and they followed him to the back bedroom.

"Everything is in the dresser, fam," 45 said with no signs of fear.

Paco checked the drawers to see nothing, until he pulled out the bottom shelf to see stacks of money.

"There's a duffle bag in the closet, Paco," 45 said, surprising them that he knew their names.

"I guess you know my name too?" Kazzy asked.

"Kazzy Loc, but that shit don't mean shit, bro. Y'all niggas do what y'all do," 45 told Kazzy in a cocky tone. Kazzy shot 45 in the head with his gun then helped Paco bag up the $400,000 that was for Big Blazer, but it was now theirs.

***

Canon USP Prison, PA

D Fatal Brim was in his cell on lock-down because there was a ten-man fight on the other side of the prison. Dudes from Texas crushed out with the Midwest dudes, and a couple of prisoners got stabbed.

When the jail went on these types of lock-downs, D Fatal Brim would work on his case motions so he could get back in court, because he felt as if he didn't have a fair trial at court.

He was reading a hood novel by Lock Down Publications and Ca$h Presents called *Life of a Savage* by Romell Tukes. He loved books and he had all of the author's books in his cell.

D Fatal Brim's neighbor knocked on his wall asking for a soup, and D Fatal Brim told him he would send him some food over when the CO made his rounds.

Chapter 32

Trey Side, BX

Blu hung up the phone, standing next to his car thinking if he should go out with Bugatti Boy, who was on his way to a club. The club scene wasn't Blu's thing too much. He'd rather be in the hood getting money with his crew.

Two of his shooters came out of the building ready to go outta town to a party on a college campus in Utica, NY.

"What's shaking, Blu," one of the young soldiers stated.

"Ain't shit, bro, you know the vibes. Where y'all going?" Blu saw they both were rocking Gucci outfits and fake Rolexes.

"A college party. You tryna pull up? We got wild hoes on deck," the tall, ugly one stated.

"Nah, I'ma pass, bro. I gotta go meet Bugatti Boy at some club, but I'ma get up with y'all in a couple of days, you heard." When Blu turned around, it was too late. A bullet ripped through his left shoulder blade.

"Ahhhhhahhhh!" Blu screamed in pain, clutching his shoulder.

Bloc
Bloc
Bloc

Blu's two hitters covered him, going at it with the four gunmen across the street in front of the laundromat.

Bloc
Bloc
Bloc
Bloc

Blu was now in war mode, shooting back hitting one of the gunmen in his neck and stomach.

"Look out, Dash!" Blu shouted, seeing Lil' Blazer had the drop on his young boy.

Lil' Blazer's bullets slammed into Dash's head, dropping him. When Blu saw that, he went crazy with his pistol. Two more of Lil'

Blazer's men got hit up in Blu's crossfire, but Blu's little homie caught one of his wild bullets also.

When Blu saw he killed his little homie, he stopped shooting as Lil' Blazer was already gone. Blu got in his car, leaving his young boy dead in a pool of blood.

***

Salsa Con Fuego Lounge, BX

Bugatti Boy was having the time of his life with two sexy Puerto Rican chicks dancing on him in the middle of the club. Karol G's song played in the club by the DJ, who was turned up for Latina night in the club every Thursday.

Bugatti Boy loved coming to Salsa Con Fuego because the women were sexy and ready to do whatever. After almost an hour of dancing, Bugatti Boy was drained. He walked to the bar area with both women laughing and on his arms.

"Papi, let's go to an after-hour spot in Washington Heights."

Bugatti Boy looked at the slim, cute mami like she lost her mind, because his feet were already hurting in his Louis Vuitton's.

"Aight, but what we doing after that?" Bugatti Boy saw both women smile and laugh as if he said something funny.

"Don't worry about that, we gonna take good care of you," one of them whispered into his ear while rubbing his semi-hard penis.

Bugatti Boy led them out of the crowded club. He had a feeling tonight was going to be a long night.

"You drove, papi? We took an Uber," one of the women stated.

"I got the red Benz over there," he said, walking down the stairs of the club.

"Damn, you ballin'."

"Nah, I'm just living," he corrected her, seeing a shadow.

Bloc. . .

Bloc. . .

Bugatti shot first at the two shooters he saw trying to get him out the way.

Boc

Boc

Boc

Boc

YG shot back, missing Bugatti Boy but hitting one of the Spanish women in her heart and lungs. The other woman yelled, trying to cater to her girlfriend and best friend, until two bullets split her head up.

Bugatti Boy leaned against a small motorcycle, firing at YG and his shooter while dodging bullets at the same time.

"Shit, son." Bugatti had six shots left and no extra clip except in his car, which was 20 feet away.

A car pulled up and it was Blu. He parked in the middle of the street and jumped out with a Draco, hitting YG's shooter at least six times and YG in his wrist, making YG turn to run.

Bugatti hopped in his car and followed Blu. He was happy his boy showed up at the right time, but he knew if he didn't, he would have been dead.

Romell Tukes

Chapter 33

Kingbridge, BX

Banger was in some bitch's crib he recently met, fucking her brains out in her bedroom. The room was hot with no fan or AC, so the window was open.

"Ugghhh, fuck, Banger, I love you!" the woman shouted, even though she'd just met him days ago.

Sherly's pussy was small and hollow for a skinny chick, but it was wet. Banger had her legs in the air going to work, pounding her pussy out the frame.

"Oh my god, take some out, daddy, you hurting me."

"Bitch, shut up and take this dick!" Banger yelled.

"Ok, mmmm..." She placed the pillow over her mouth, letting him kill her guts until he nutted inside of her.

She had a small, little butt, so when he flipped her over, he went deep into her sex box, making her spread her cheeks open.

"Yesssss, daddyyyy!" she screamed, climaxing on his dick.

They both were unaware of the man creeping into the bedroom window from the fire escape.

Banger was deep in her hairy pussy when he saw the room darken from the outside morning light. When he looked back, he saw Lil' Blazer standing there with a gun pointed at him.

Banger left his gun in the car, so he knew it was over, but he continued to fuck Sherly until he filled her pussy hole up with his cum.

"Sherly, I see you still a thot," Lil' Blazer told his ex-girlfriend, who left him when he went upstate to prison years ago.

"Lil' Blazer!" She covered herself, scared to death.

Lil' Blazer had been following Banger for a day, and when he saw him go to Sherly's crib, he couldn't believe his eyes. He used to sneak in her mom's house window all the time to fuck Sherly, so he knew how to get inside.

"Yeah, it's me, surprise." Lil' Blazer saw the fear on her face.

"Suck my dick, nigga. You got one up on us, but we ten up," Banger said strongly.

"I'm glad you feel that way, my G." Lil' Blazer raised his pistol.

Boc

Boc

Boc

Boc

The shots entered Banger's chest with ease, killing him, but Lil' Blazer wasn't done. He shot Sherly five times in her face for all the hurt and pain she put him through.

"Dirty bitch," Lil' Blazer mumbled before leaving out the window. Sherly's mom was deaf, so she couldn't hear what was going on.

***

Burnside, BX
Two Weeks Later

Banger's funeral was a small one, mostly his homies and family members, but there were only thirty-five people there to show their support. Red and her beautiful mom were in tears the whole time, seeing Banger in his casket with his arms crossed.

Lil' K was there to comfort Red. They were now dealing with each other on a higher level. Their lust and passion for each other was bottled up for so long, but now it was out and the vibes were crazy.

Lil' K and Blu saw a truck parked on the lower side of the graveyard. Today was a rainy day outside, so it was muddy and the clouds were dark gray.

"You see that?" Blu whispered in Lil' K's ear.

"Facts, you strapped?" Lil' K replied.

"Yeah." Blu knew what time it was as they walked off, leaving everybody to mourn.

Red saw Lil' K and Blu walk off, and she knew they were up to something, but she had to comfort her mom. She knew she was heartbroken.

***

Dollar's truck was parked at the lower level of the graveyard, and he was thinking if he should shoot up the little get together or just let them grieve.

When he saw Lil' K and Blu walking his way, he wondered if they saw him, because he was parked behind a tree in the cut. The closer they got to Dollar, he pulled out his MP5 and lowered his window, but before he could get the barrel out the window, shots went off.

Bugatti Boy shot out his back windows, almost taking off his ear. Now Lil' K and Blu were airing out his truck, hitting him in his leg. Dollar was trapped. He was able to start the car and get out of there, but the bullets he caught were very painful.

Lil' K saw Dollar before he raced off and vowed to get him, if it was the last thing he did. Nobody knew who killed Banger yet, but now Lil' K thought it was Dollar, or someone from his camp.

Romell Tukes

Chapter 34

Bridgeport, CT

Dollar had plans to take Cameron out on a nice boat cruise for the weekend. He knew she would like it. He needed a getaway anyway, with everything he had going on in the streets trying to hunt niggas down.

"Babe, you ready?" Dollar yelled upstairs, standing at the bottom ready to leave because the cruise ship left in less than an hour.

"Here I come." Cameron walked down the stairs in a beautiful white dress, looking like an angel.

"You're looking wonderful." Dollar loved the way she could switch it up and change her style.

"I'm ready." She smiled, walking out the door, giving him a good look at her ass bouncing as she went to the car.

"What you got planned for us, baby? I'm glad we can finally spend some time together. I've been gone for the past couple of weeks with my family, so shit's been exhausting for me, but all I could think about was you, Paco, I swear," Cameron said, unaware of her slip up.

Dollar was quiet because this was the third time she'd called him Paco's name, but what he didn't understand was outta all the niggas in the world, why would she call him his enemy's name?

"I'm glad you back, baby, but I've been meaning to ask you something." Dollar drove onto the interstate.

"Sure, what's up, baby?"

"That tattoo you have on your left upper shoulder, whose name is that?" Dollar had been wanting to ask her that question for some time now.

"Oh, that's my mom's name," Cameron told him, wondering why he was tripping.

"So, you and your mom have the same name?" He caught her off guard.

"Huh?"

"So, both of your names are Hasley. I saw it on your ID." Dollar pulled over and saw her reaching into her purse.

Dollar was quick on the draw.

"Bitch, don't fucking move." Dollar placed his gun at her head. "Who the fuck are you, and who sent you, Paco?"

"Fuck you, I sent myself," Hasley said, upset at herself for slipping so hard.

Hasley didn't tell Paco she was going on this mission. She wanted to show Paco she was a killer just like him. She thought by using the name Cameron, he would fall head over heels for her, especially with her looks.

"You want to play those games, ok. One last time, who sent you?" Dollar was running outta patience.

"Fuck you, nigga, my heart don't pump fear. Paco's gonna kill you anyway, bitch ass nigga," Hasley spit.

Bloc. . .

Bloc. . .

Bloc. . .

Dollar shot her a couple of times in her face, then got out the car and dragged her body into a small ditch on the side of the highway.

***

Mott Haven, BX

YG and his little homie walked down the block to the corner store to buy some dutch masters to roll up some loud in. The past couple of weeks, YG had been in his hood getting to a bag. He was locking down his side of the city with Lil' Blazer's help.

YG's main focus was getting money and trying to stay alive, because he had so much beef he didn't know which way it was coming from.

Lil' Blazer's main thing was killing Kazzy Loc and Lil' K's crew. YG tried to explain to Lil' Blazer that Kazzy wasn't an easy target. He played the cat and mouse game. YG knew to kill Kazzy and his crew, they would need to have real patience, but Lil' Blazer was too thirsty.

They walked into the local corner store.

"What's up, papi?" YG spoke to the older Dominican man who ran the corner store for about two decades now.

"YG, how you been?" the older man said, watching YG's friend, who always stole something. "Tell sticky fingers he better pay for the Snickers he put in his pocket."

"I'ma pay for it." YG went to the cooler to grab a soda.

The store owner did something to the front door then came back around the counter. YG or his soldier didn't peep the movement.

YG and his boy paid for everything at the counter.

"Before you go..." The Dominican went under his chair and pulled out his shotgun and whistled.

Paco came out the back with a weapon in his hand, seeing the crazy look on YG's face. The store owner was good friends with Paco's family. He used to fuck with his aunty.

"About time," YG said before Paco shot him eight times. YG's friend tried to run, but the store's door was locked. Paco shot him five times in his back, killing him also. The store owner cleaned up the bloody mess and re-opened the store in an hour.

Romell Tukes

Chapter 35

Atlanta, Zone 6

Big Blazer stood in a parking lot with a couple of his homies, dressed in all red. Big Blazer was a Blood and everybody was Sex, Money, Murder, the same set as him.

With everything going on in New York, Big Blazer knew coming to Atlanta was the perfect getaway. The nigga who ran the hood was a close friend of Big Blazer's, so when Big Blazer made him an offer to flood his hood with the best coke he'd ever seen, it was over from there.

"Ay, shawty, you was in the club last night wilding. You tossed about $100,000. I had like ten of dem hoes ask me if you was a rapper," Fioso said, making Big Blazer laugh as he thought about how he turned up in club Blue Flame last night.

"I took three of them bitches back to my condo downtown last night, son. That shit was a night to remember," Big Blazer bragged. He was fucking three bitches last night for hours off the molly. Big Blazer wasn't heavy on drugs, but he let the dancers talk him into it.

The drug traffic was slow, but when niggas came to cop weight, it was a brick or better.

***

Washington Height, NY

The news of Hasley's death hit the news, and Paco's cousin called him asking about the chick he used to be with. When Paco asked him what about her, he told Paco there was a chick on the news who looked just like her.

Paco hadn't heard from Hasley in a couple of days, but he knew she was upset because of her miscarriage she recently had.

Turning on the news fucked his head up seeing Hasley's body being found in a ditch near CT. It crushed his heart to the core.

He couldn't figure out why she would be in Connecticut, then it hit him. Paco knew Dollar lived out there, so he knew it was a direct hit.

***

White Plains, NY

Monore got done shopping at the mall in the Gallery. She picked up something for her man, Lil' Blazer, who she'd been dealing with for a couple of months now. She knew she wasn't the only one, but as long as she was top two, it was cool with her.

Monore was very thick, with juicy thighs, a big ass, skinny waist, cute face, short hair, and tattoos. Her car was fucked up, so she'd been using Lil' Blazer's red Benz to get around.

Walking out the third floor level through the garage, all she could think about was going back to Lil' Blazer's to dress up for him and fuck the shit outta him. There wasn't too much he could do with his micro size, but she aimed to please.

A cute female got out of a GMC SUV with skinny jeans and a hoodie. Monore was never into females, but she had to admit, she was a bad little bitch.

The chick with the hoodie on walked up to Monore and went in her hoodie front pocket.

Bloc. . .
Bloc. . .
Bloc . . .

Red fired three holes into Monore's chest, killing her right where she stood. Red saw the job was done and got ghost in the truck back to the Bronx.

***

Parkchester, BX

Hours Later

"Bro, you really wifed Red, that's crazy." Blu shook his head, knowing those two together were dangerous.

"Yeah, that shit was bound to happen," Lil' K told him, pulling up to the block where their lick was.

"Ain't that like fucking your bro or a man? Because she acts like us," Blu said.

"What? Nigga, you tripping, her shit wet and on another level, facts, and she can suck a mean dick." Lil' K was surprised at how much of a freak she was.

"Too much information, but that's the boy coming out the crib with a bookbag." Blu saw Trio coming out a building.

"We gotta get him now." Lil' K jumped out.

Trio was on his phone when he was ambushed. Lil' K snatched his book bag from his shoulder. Trio was a weed and pill plug. He was on his way to re-up with $250,000, but that was over now.

"Take the money. I don't want no smoke," Trio said, before Blu shot him six times in his stomach.

Lil' K and the crew were $250,000 richer, but they were on their way to Long Island to hit another lick Kritty set up for them the other night.

Chapter 36

Highbridge, BX

Today, Kazzy Loc's wifey, Ulissa, was having a party for her birthday in a nice-size ballroom. There were all types of people there from the Bronx, and Ulissa's family from DR was also there. Ulissa wore a nice red designer outfit with heels and had her hair done. She was the center of attention the whole day.

"I can't wait to show you what I got as a surprise for you," Kazzy told her in her ear.

"I hear you, papi, but how about I give you a surprise now," she replied.

"Oh, yeah, I'm wit' that." He followed her outside the party to the car lot.

Kazzy Loc was so focused on Ulissa's ass, he ain't see the two gunmen hop out from a few cars over. By the time he saw the two gunmen, it was too late.

"Ulissa!" Kazzy shouted as he looked back, to see her catching two bullets to her chest, dropping.

Lil' Blazer fired rounds at Kazzy, who was ducking, trying to get to Ulissa, but the bullets made it hard.

Boc
Boc
Boc
Boc
Boc
Boc

Kazzy fired back, hitting Lil' Blazer's man twice in his forehead.

BOOM
BOOM

Lil' Blazer ran to the other side of the lot once he saw six shooters run out the ballroom with guns. Kazzy continued to shoot at Lil' Blazer until he was long gone.

Everybody ran to Ulissa's aid, but she was already lifeless and dead. Kazzy had real tears in his eyes. He left the scene before the police arrived, feeling empty.

***

Sux 2 Prison, VA

Knight had a job in the kitchen to burn some of his time and to stay out the unit. Doing prison time in a different state was harder than he could imagine, but luckily, there were lots of New York niggas in the prison.

Knight worked in the back warehouse and unloaded trucks when they arrived every Tuesday and Thursday. Today, he was there alone, besides the regular CO chick, who was a thick, country white girl with blonde hair.

"Can you come with me to get some boxes for dinner?" the female CO asked Knight, who was chilling on his break.

"Sure." Knight followed her to the back closet.

Once the door closed, the female CO attacked Knight, pulling out his manhood and getting on her knees.

Knight couldn't even move. He couldn't believe this was happening. He heard stories about female COs fucking prisoners, but never did he think he'd be one. Knight always caught her staring at him, but he paid it no mind.

The way she was sucking his pole, he wanted to cry. She was working him, sucking, jerking, and spitting. Before he was about to bust in her mouth, she stopped and bent over, pulling down her pants.

Her pussy was hairy, but when he slid into her, she was warm and tight.

"Ugghh, yessss, fuck me with that big black cock!" she screamed.

He was bouncing on her big ass, spreading her ass cheeks, going deeper in her love box.

"I'm about cum on this big cock, yess, oh my god!" she yelled, cumming at the same time as him.

When he pulled out, he was dripping with her juices. She put his dick in her mouth and sucked him off until he was dry with nothing left.

"Thank you," she said, leaving, fixing her clothes.

Knight's legs were shaky, but he got himself together and walked back into the kitchen with the other workers. He saw the CO bitch in a group of male COs' faces laughing and saying black jokes.

Later on that night, he went back to his unit.

"Yo, let me holler at you, bro," Knight told Don, his celly who was watching the world news with other prisoners.

"What's up, dawg?" Don walked in their cell.

"I just fucked that thick bitch that works in the kitchen," Knight bragged.

"Nah, bruh, that blondie, racist bitch?"

"Yeah, factz, son."

"Damn, how was it?" Don asked as Knight spent a whole hour breaking down the scene that took place.

Romell Tukes

Chapter 37

Third Ave, Bronx

The nice, sunny day gave the city a good evening vibe as shoppers flooded the Third Ave shopping area.

Blu and Bugatti were parked across the street in a Jeep truck watching a tattoo parlor. The tattoo parlor was owned by a young hustler named KB, from Long Island. KB wasn't just the owner of the shop, but he was also a plug.

He'd been selling keys of raw coke out his shop since it first opened last year in the middle of the busiest location in the Bronx.

"You think he in there, bro?" Bugatti asked Blu, who was on his phone texting a new little bitch he recently met. The girl he was texting was the one who put him on to KB's status, unaware Blu was a true jack boy.

"What you say?"

"Damn, bro, you be acting real funny sometimes." Bugatti shook his head because he and Blu used to be real close, but lately, Bugatti had been seeing Blu act distant towards him only.

"Nah, son, my mind be everywhere at times. I don't know about you, Bugatti, but I love these streets to death, but I'm not try-ing to die in them, you heard," Blu said, being honest.

"We gonna die anyway," Bugatti shot back.

"Yeah, but I wanna die of cancer or something, bro. I lost my mother to these streets, and the only nigga I ever looked up to is a fucking rat now, hidden out somewhere," Blu said, referring to his brother, Black.

"I feel you, bro. That's why I'm living day for day."

"Factz," Blu replied.

"The shop looks empty. Let's just run up in there and put eve-rybody in zip ties," Bugatti said.

"Aight." Blu hopped out, unaware of the man who got out his car parked a couple of cars behind them.

***

Bankroll saw both men get out of the Jeep, about to walk into the street as traffic breezed past.

Boc...

Boc...

Boc...

Boc...

Bankroll sent shots at both men, who were on point and got their weapons out to fire back.

Bloc...

Bloc...

Blu hit Bankroll in his upper thigh, making him fall and drop his gun under his car. When Bugatti saw Bankroll's gun slide under his car, he was sending shots at Bankroll, who made it back inside his car.

Bloc

Bloc

Bloc

Blu and Bugatti fired multiple rounds at Bankroll's car, which was speeding off. The two men got in the Jeep, racing off, upset Bankroll just fucked up their sweet lick.

***

South Broadway, BX

Paco and Kazzy Loc drove in the older Cadillac sedan model, both in their own thoughts, with one of Big Blazer's workers in the trunk zip-tied up.

Since Kazzy lost Ulissa, he'd been emotionally detached. Losing her was like losing his mother. Every day he felt like it was his fault that his mom or Ulissa wasn't here anymore.

"What's on your mind, son?" Paco asked, knowing his friend like the back of his hand.

"I've been thinking, and I want to come together with my brother and his crew. We need them and they need us. Regardless,

Lil' K is still family and Knight gonna be home soon, so I know he would want it like this anyway. Less locked up, Black a snitch ducked off, shit is all bad." Kazzy drove into a wooded area.

"I agree, they could be useful. They saved my ass before, and we beefing with the same people," Paco shared, giving in, because at first, he disliked Lil' K's crew, but after seeing how they moved, he was very impressed.

"This the first time you agree on something," Kazzy stated, parking the car.

"Factz," Paco said, following his lead.

When they popped the trunk, a fat man was tied up, crying with his mouth taped. Paco took the tape off his mouth.

"Look, I got whatever you need. I'm not ready to die," the man cried.

"Where is Big Blazer?" Kazzy asked.

"He just got back from Atlanta. He's been at this whore house in Washington Heights he been running," the fat man cried.

"On what block?" Paco asked.

"I believe on Post."

"Perfect." Kazzy looked at Paco then shot the fat nigga seven times in his chest before tossing his heavy body onto the grassy area.

"This nigga in a whore house. What the fuck he doing, pimpin'?" Paco was confused.

"Or tricking." Kazzy laughed, getting back in the car.

Chapter 38

Washington Heights, NY

Big Blazer sat on the toilet in the bathroom getting his dick sucked by two young, slim, pretty Dominican women fresh from DR.

Since he'd been back in New York, he hadn't been to the Bronx. He'd been chilling in Heights. His people, Big GT, gave him his own whore house he could sell his drugs out of and have women fulfill whatever he needed.

"You like that, papi?" one of the women said, looking at him while sucking the tip of his dick while the other woman traced her tongue around the shaft.

The sounds of loud slurping and spitting filled the room. Big Blazer had no clue both women were minors. The way they took turns deep throating his whole dick, he wasn't thinking about their age.

There were two more women in the living room area busting down keys Big Blazer just got from his plug, Fats, earlier. Holiday was supposed to come pick up the drugs in a few hours, so he wanted everything to be in place.

"Swallow that dick, bitch," Big Blazer said as one of the women was sucking his dick fast, going crazy on his pipe.

The sounds of gunfire took him out of his trance of cumming. Big Blazer's gun was in the living room.

The bathroom door was open, so he grabbed both women by their hair as they screamed. He tossed both women into the hallway, to see Paco and Kazzy making their way towards him.

Boc. . .

Boc. . .

Boc. . .

Boc. . .

Big Blazer dodged the bullets and locked the bathroom door as both women were on the floor, shot.

There was a bathroom window, and he had no choice but to make his exit ass naked, because his clothes were next door. He came in the bathroom to take a shower and have a threesome.

By the time Paco and Kazzy busted into the bathroom, Big Blazer was running down the street ass naked in the chilly day.

"Shit, how the fuck we let that happen?" Paco shouted, leaving the crib. Kazzy knew he would have a chance again to run into Big Blazer.

***

MillBrook Projects, BX

Lil' K and the whole crew were on the playground tonight, drinking and speaking on future plans and licks.

"What's up, baby, why you so quiet?" Lil' K looked at Red, who was looking cute and sexy. Since she'd been fucking Lil' K, she stopped dressing like a boy and did regular girl shit, except dresses and heels.

The only time she dressed up was for him during sex or to please him. She was beyond in love with Lil' K. Anytime she wasn't around him, she would go crazy.

The sex was amazing. He was the only male she ever made love to. When her father used to rape her, she used to promise herself to never let a nigga enter her again. That changed with Lil' K, because she was thirsty to fuck and suck his dick.

"I'm good, just watching that Benz coupe over there," she said as he looked through the lot, paying it no mind. Red was always his ears.

"Everybody strapped, so we good. Let them niggas pull up, you heard." Lil' K took a gulp out the bottle of Henny.

***

"You sure you wanna do this?" Paco asked Kazzy.

"Yeah." Kazzy got out the Benz with his chain swinging on his neck.

Paco was behind him when they walked into the small playground area where Lil' K's crew was staring at them both as if they were lost.

"Yo, Lil' K, I need to holler at you real quick, bro," Kazzy asked his little brother, who didn't move at first.

"I'll be back," Lil' K told his crew.

"This shit getting outta hand. What the fuck is your problem with me?" Kazzy was upset as he spoke his mind when they were outta earshot distance.

"Nigga, y'all got Mommy killed, and y'all niggas all for self. We supposed to be family, but you and Knight blinded by greed and a green piece of paper. Me and mine getting it out the mud," Lil' K stated, trying to control his temper.

Red heard Lil' K's voice getting loud and was on point, because he never yelled.

"You right, and I'm sorry, bro. The streets had me forgetting what my purpose was and to put family first. I'm not perfect, bro, but I need you and your crew. We stronger together, as you see." Kazzy looked at Lil' K's team.

"Just because you blood and I understand where you coming from, I'ma ask my crew." Lil' K walked off and spoke to his crew for five minutes.

Lil' K walked to Kazzy and Paco, smiling.

"It's lite, but y'all niggas better not cross us." Lil' K's smile got serious before walking off. Kazzy knew this was a new start.

Romell Tukes

Chapter 39

Queens, NY

Natalie worked in Club Atlantis. She was a beautiful Puerto Rican and Black woman with a killer all-natural body. She was a bartender at the new club, but tonight, she was a bottle girl because they were short staffed.

Her ass hung out her net outfit she wore over the two-piece G-string bikini she was killing. Tonight was a busy night. Two well-known rappers were in the building with their crew.

Natalie was so busy running back and forth to the VIP sections, she couldn't even speak to her fans, stalkers, or people she knew.

She was from Brooklyn on Church Ave, but now she had a nice home in Queens with her daughter, who was five years old. With a deadbeat baby father who was a kingpin, she thought he would at least be some type of help, but that was out of the question.

Having a baby with Fats was the worst decision she ever made in her 30 years on Earth. After having his child, she found out she was one of many baby mothers he had. To make ends meet, she had to come back to the club scene and get to a big bag.

Natalie saw a sexy, young woman sitting at the bar alone watching the dancers twerk on the stage to the City Girls' "Twerk" song.

"Hey, you good?" Natalie asked the woman.

"Yeah, I'm just waiting for someone," the woman replied.

"Ok, just wanted to say hey." Natalie never was into women, but there was something about the lady's voice, colorful eyes, and beauty that got her pussy soaked.

It was getting late, so Natalie finished up her shift and got out of the way. Most of the dancers went back home, to hotel parties, or home with one of the clients to sell some pussy. Some women would do anything for a bag, but Natalie wasn't with selling herself short.

Walking out the club to her Honda Civic, she heard someone yelling trying to get her attention, but she kept walking. She had four stalkers who would always follow her outside when the club closed, so she kept her pepper spray.

The voice sounded like a female's, so she turned around to see the sexy chick she saw sitting at the bar. Natalie had never ate pussy, but she thought tonight may be that night.

"Hey, you," Natalie stated, seeing the woman approach her with something shiny in her hand.

Bloc
Bloc
Bloc
Bloc

Red shot her in the face and ran down the block to her car and raced off. Kazzy put them on to the main problem, Fats, so they made plans to get everybody out the way.

***

MillBrook Projects, BX

It was 11 p.m. and Lil' K went into the back building with a duffle bag full of coke for his workers. What Lil' K didn't see was the eyes in the deep end of the parking lot watching him closely.

Bankroll had been parked here almost a whole day waiting for Lil' K or anybody from his crew to show up, and it finally happened.

He got out of his car so he could lay on Lil' K, so when he came back out, Bankroll could have the drop on him. When he closed his car door, he heard a little noise behind him, making him turn around.

"Act like you wanna move, bitch ass nigga, that's on crip, I'ma blow your shit off," Kazzy Loc said in a serious tone.

"I ain't scared, bro. Today just my day, fam." Bankroll knew it was over.

"I'm glad you see shit how I do, but you had a long run." Kazzy respected Bankroll's gangsta, because he was one of the harder targets until Kazzy mastered his thinking.

Kazzy Loc knew Bankroll would come to Lil' K's turf to get him, because Lil' K was moving around too much, but he still had money flowing in his hood. Kazzy Loc knew that alone would bring Bankroll to him, and it did.

"You put a lot of fear in these niggas, all of your brothers, but I remained solid!" Bankroll shouted, upset he got caught slipping.

Bankroll could have caught Lil' K last week with Red, but he chose to wait for the perfect time.

"That's a fact, but your time here is up, my G."

Boc

Boc

Boc

Boc

Boc

Kazzy Loc gave him all dome shots before getting in his truck to go meet Paco across town.

Romell Tukes

Chapter 40

Soundview, BX

Today was Thanksgiving and the crowd was out in the football field near Soundview Projects. Every year, niggas from the projects would throw a big football game and give away turkeys and school supplies.

Normally, Big Blazer was the star quarterback, but this year he was out of town. The quarterback tossed the football down the field for a Hail Mary pass.

***

"I don't see that big funny nigga." Red was looking out the car tints towards the football field.

"Me neither," Kazzy Loc said, looking on the field for Big Blazer.

Kazzy knew Soundview niggas threw a big football game on Thanksgiving every year. He told Red to come with him to look for Big Blazer, and the rest of the crew had the drop on Lil' Blazer, so they were focused on him.

Kazzy Loc knew Red and Lil' K were in a relationship. He was proud of his little brother, because Red was a dime piece. Red's beauty stood out from most chicks, and she had a gangsta swag that would turn on any real thug.

"Thanks for coming out. I wanted to spend some time with you because I want to see where your head is at, especially with the way you got my little brother's head fucked up," Kazzy Loc told her, seeing her blush at the name of Lil' K.

"My head is in the right place, and I love Lil' K with all my heart, so you have nothing to worry about." Red got serious.

"I hope not, because under Lil' K's tough skin, he's emotional with a soft heart. I can tell the way he looks at you that he really loves you." Kazzy Loc knew Lil' K better than anybody on this earth.

"Lil' K is basically my first love, and I'll never do anything to hurt him. I'm not that type of chick at all, Kazzy. Trust me, Lil' K got my heart," she admitted.

"I believe you, but what you wanna do since Big Blazer not here?" Kazzy asked her.

"Follow my lead. Let's give them a Thanksgiving to remember," Red stated, grabbing the AR-15 out the backseat and getting out the car.

Tat, tat, tat, tat, tat, tat, tat, tat, tat, tat, tat, tat...

Red and Kazzy Loc opened fire on the football game as people ran and some got hit. One minute of non-stop shooting led to three dead bodies, and eight people got seriously wounded.

When Red and Kazzy left, he was impressed with Red's boldness and gunplay. Kazzy knew Lil' K found an official chick, and she got his stamp of approval.

***

Mount Vernon, NY

Lil' Blazer spent his Thanksgiving at his new girl's mom's house, who lived in a nice area in Mount Vernon. Catie's mom was white and her dad was black. Her dad was a Mount Vernon cop and strict on his daughter. Catie told her dad Lil' Blazer was a college student at her college, and he believed his daughter.

Having Lil' Blazer meet her parents was big to her, and to Catie's surprise, her parents liked him. They were all eating and having a good time, telling jokes and stories of Catie's childhood.

***

"You sure this is the house, Kritty?" Lil' K asked, looking at the nice yellow house in the middle of an upper-class neighborhood.

"Yeah, cuz, that's a fact. Catie used to fuck with my little homie, and she post up Lil' Blazer on social media at her house, cuz.

I'm telling you, he in there," Kritty stated while Lil' K saw Lil' Blazer's red Benz coupe.

"We about to find out." Lil' K got out and walked the street with Kritty behind him.

Kritty was a pro at breaking into someone's crib, so they got inside in minutes.

Walking inside the polished, carpeted home, he heard voices from the dining room area. When he walked into the area, Catie's father jumped up, but Lil' K shot him twice in the head, knocking him back down.

"Ahhhhhhh!" Catie's mom yelled, before Kritty shot her four times in her breast.

Lil' Blazer stared at Lil' K. He didn't even have his gun on him, he left it in the car.

"Any last words?" Lil' K asked, but before Lil' Blazer could reply, his bullets silenced him.

Kritty shot Catie, killing her instantly, before walking out the crib.

"I told you, cuz, but that bitch pops was the chief of police," Kritty told Lil' K, who shrugged his shoulders.

Romell Tukes

Chapter 41

Brooklyn, NY

"I like to work alone, but due to our new situation, I'm willing to bend my rules," Paco told Bugatti Boy, who paid him no attention, listening to rap music playing on the stereo, Hot 97.

Paco and Bugatti were on a mission to rob an African heroin plug in the RedHook section of Brooklyn.

"You talk too much," Bugatti Boy said, resting his head on the headrest of the BMW.

"Y'all young niggas these days can't soak up game nowadays. Everybody got a complex these days," Paco shot back, watching the roads for potholes.

"I ain't got not complex, son. I just don't take wisdom from anybody." Bugatti Boy always listened to helpful advice, but he knew niggas like Paco just liked to hear themselves talk a lot.

"I feel you, bro, but who put you on to this plug nigga?" Paco asked.

"I know people who know people," he shot back, in his own thoughts.

"This shit don't seem to be accurate, playboy, but if I sense any funny shit, I'ma kill you."

"Be my guest." Bugatti Boy looked out the car window into the dark sky, hoping what he was about to do was the right thing for his crew.

***

Saint guided the large blue commercial van into the private warehouse with six armed goons behind him. In the van was tons of dope inside big can containers shipped from Africa, where Saint got his dope from. He supplied New York, New Jersey, and Delaware. He was big time.

Saint was a big African man who grew up in the mean streets of Brooklyn. Being one of the biggest dope suppliers was hard without going to prison or being set up by rats.

Luckily, Saint always stayed two steps ahead of people and kept a low profile. Before the warehouse doors closed, shots went off, distracting everybody.

Bloc. . .

Bloc. . .

Bloc. . .

Saint's goons fired back with their machine guns at the two gunmen dressed in all black.

Tat. . .

Tat. . .

Bloc. . .

Bloc. . .

Saint got hit in his kneecap, dropping him, while the rest of his goons soon fell dead after him. When Bugatti and Paco saw all the men were dead, they approached Saint, who was crying in pain.

"You don't know what you're about to do, just leave now while you can," Saint said, holding his shattered knee.

Bloc

Bloc

Bloc

Bloc

Bugatti Boy killed Saint and looked in the van to see it was filled with big can containers.

"I'ma take this, you follow," Bugatti Boy said as Paco couldn't believe what he saw in the back. This may have been the biggest lick he ever saw.

Paco wondered how could a little nigga like Bugatti Boy be aware of a big lick like this. Even though the crew was financially set, Paco would never turn down free bands.

***

Uptown, BX

Rochell was in a Tahoe truck grinding on a young nigga's lap as she rode his dick up and down.

"Uhhhggg, yess, fuck me!" Rochell screamed as Mole grabbed her big ass.

Mole couldn't take it, her pussy was so wet and tight, he couldn't keep up with her. She was fucking the shit outta him.

"I'm about to cum, baby, go deeper," she moaned while Mole sucked on her big titties like a baby.

Rochell was Big Blazer's mom and a true freak. She loved young niggas like Mole, who was twenty years old. Mole worked for Big Blazer and he used to see Rochell all the time looking good, so when she threw the pussy at him earlier, he wasted no time. She was down for whatever, and Mole felt the same way.

Once she came, Rochell got off his lap and started sucking his dick with her insane head game. Mole never experienced this type of head game, as she twisted her head while deep throating, doing all types of nasty shit.

A man came up to his car window, parked in a park behind a dumpster.

Boc

Boc

Boc

Boc

Blu killed both of them before he ran off with a hard-on because Big Blazer's mom was getting down with her head game.

Romell Tukes

Chapter 42

Sux 2 Prison, VA

Six Months Later

Knight looked at the sky and perfect clouds, saying a quick prayer that he made it outta prison. Being free felt so good, he wanted to cry as he waited at the bus stop next to the prison.

He had a bus pass to take him to a New York bus station. Last week, he wrote to Kazzy Loc and Lil' K, telling them he was getting out today.

Knight had been out of the loop with what's been going on in New York because he didn't want any extra stress while being in jail. He wanted to stay focused in the belly of the beast.

Luckily, Paco sent him a Gucci outfit he could leave the jail in with his black Timbs. The clothes were a very tight fit because he gained a lot of muscle from lifting weights.

His dreads were hanging down his back and his grill was shining. He also grew out his beard, making him look like a Muslim.

The Greyhound bus came and he got on, ready to go back home. VA left a bad taste in his mouth.

***

42nd St., New York City
Eight Hours Later

Knight got off the bus at a busy bus station, making his way to a local ATM machine down the street. The first thing he planned to do while in his cell was visit his mom's grave, because he didn't have a chance yet due to being locked up.

After getting five hundred dollars out of the ATM machine, he took an Uber to the Bronx to visit his mom's tombstone. While being in prison, Knight tried to block the thoughts out his head about his mom's murder.

He felt like it was his fault his mom was dead. Knight's biggest fear being in the streets was bringing his drama to his loved one's door steps.

Being locked up cleared his mind and helped him think straight. Robbing would always be in his heart. He was a true jack boy, but Knight now saw a bigger picture.

While most niggas sold their souls to get rich, Knight knew how to get it out the mud. Now with a Miami plug, he wanted to take over the drug trade. He was going to leave jacking to the young niggas.

***

Bronx, NY

Less than thirty minutes later, the Uber pulled up to the grave-yard. It was still a little light outside as the purple and orange skyline rose over the city.

Walking to his mom's tombstone felt like walking down death row, cell block six. His knees started to get weak.

When he saw his mom's name on the tombstone, tears that he'd been holding on to for years quickly left his eyes.

"I'm sorry, Mom. This is all my fault. I wish it was me there instead of you. Lord knows you didn't deserve to die," Knight spoke loudly, as if he was talking to someone.

"I'ma take care of Kazzy, Lil' K, and BeBe, I swear," Knight stated, wiping his tears.

"Nigga, you better take care of us, cry baby," Kazzy Loc said, walking up behind him with Lil' K on his side.

Knight hugged both of his brothers tightly, giving them no room to breathe.

"We miss you too, nigga, damn," Lil' K repeated, fixing his designer chain.

"How y'all know I was here, son?" Knight wondered.

"Come on, cuz, we know you better than you know yourself," Kazzy replied.

"Oh, so y'all fools got six senses or some magical powers?" Knight said, happy to see his brothers both here and alive.

"Something like that." Lil' K put a dozen new roses on his mom's tombstone.

"Where's Paco's crazy ass? He probably in pussy." Knight knew Paco's style. He wasn't gonna pass up on some good pussy.

"Him and Blu in Atlanta paying our boy a visit," Kazzy said with an evil grin.

"Blu, who the fuck is that? And what boy?" Knight felt like he was lost.

"There's a lot you missed out on, but we gonna update you, son," Lil' K told him before they all left the graveyard.

* **

Atlanta, GA

Black came to Atlanta and changed his name to OC. He resided on the Westside of the city where he had a crew getting money.

Black knew after he ratted, the police or the witness protection program wouldn't save his life. He also missed the fast lifestyle, so he came to Atlanta with drugs and money.

It wasn't hard to find a plug in Atlanta. With the right people he came across, he was able to build his own crew.

He was on his way to a hotel in downtown Atlanta with two strippers in the Wraith with him from the club he just left. Every Thursday, he went to Magic City to turn up.

Once at the four-star hotel, he let the women pay for the room. Black walked towards the elevator.

"OC, I left my purse in the car. I'ma go get it," a sexy, thick, brown-skin woman said.

"Hurry up." Black gave her his car key and ran off.

Black and the other woman got in the elevator, but it looked like it was stuck on the top floor.

"Damn it, come on, let's take the stairs. It's only two flights. You got the condoms and molly?" Black asked the tall, ugly woman whose body was outta this world.

"Yes, daddy," she said, looking behind her out into the car lot to see her girl speeding off in OC's Wraith.

In the staircase, two men were coming down a flight, but she and Black paid them any mind until both men stopped.

"What's good, rat ass nigga?" Paco said with his gun pointed at them both.

When Black saw Paco and his brother, Blu, he thought he was dreaming.

"Blu," Black said, trying to get sympathy.

"You got my man killed, and I hate snitches." Blu's voice got cold.

Boc. . .

Boc. . .

Boc. . .

Boc. . .

Boc. . .

Blu shot his brother in his head then kicked his body down the stairs. Paco killed the stripper bitch.

Months ago, Paco came to Atlanta and saw Black in a club. Paco then started fucking one of the dancers and paid her to set Black up, and she did her job well.

Chapter 43

Uptown, Bronx

Blu pulled into a fast-food spot drive thru on a late night, fresh from Atlanta. Earlier today, he met Knight for the first time. They all had a little sit down to discuss future plans, but the main topic was money.

Knight told them he had a Miami plug and they were about to see some major paper. When he told them they didn't have to rob anymore, everybody told him he was tripping, even Kazzy Loc and Paco.

The crew explained to Knight that jacking was their way of life and it became a bad habit. Lil' K made a point, saying by robbing other drug dealers, they would eliminate all competition. Knight had to give in because everybody was against his better judgement.

Killing Black recently was hard to do, but he knew there were rules to the game, and Black violated the first rule, snitching.

Blu moved up to the intercom, unaware of the man walking up on his passenger side window.

Boc
Boc
Boc
Boc
Boc
Boc

The hot bullets all entered Blu's skull, killing him, leaving him slumped in his seat with blood stains all over the window.

Big Blazer jumped back in his all-navy blue Hellcat, racing off. Big Blazer was about to get a late-night snack then slide back to a little bitch's crib, who lived in GunHill Projects.

When he saw Blu in front of him, it was like he caught fresh fish on a line. He planned to move to North Carolina tomorrow, where he bought a nice house in Greenville.

Holiday and Head were running his drug business until he came back, but right now, the feds were in town, and going back to prison wasn't on his agenda right now.

The feds just picked up seventeen niggas from his projects, charging them with the RICO Act. Word got back to Big Blazer's homies from MDC Brooklyn federal build that a couple of niggas were telling and Big Blazer was the topic of discussion.

Getting outta town for a while was the smartest thing he knew he could do for a while until shit died down.

***

MillBrook Projects, BX
Next Day

Lil' K and Red recently got the call minutes ago from Bugatti Boy that Blu got killed last night in a drive thru uptown.

Everybody was fucked up over the news, even Kazzy and Paco, because Blu had heart and a strong personality that attracted people.

Red drove through the Bronx with Lil' K leaned back in the passenger seat with a Glock 23 pistol with a 30-round clip attached to it, looking for any ops.

"You good, daddy? I know we took a big loss, but everything's going to fall in place, just be patient, baby." Red could tell by the look on Lil' K's face he was ready to turn up, but Red was a thinker, and Lil' K thought off of emotion.

"I'm cool, you heard." His words were short. Lil' K had blood on his mind, and all he could think about was murder.

They rode through the city listening to NBA Youngboy and Kevin Gates.

***

Patterson Projects, BX

BeBe exited her car she parked in the back of her friend's building. She was about to go upstairs and drink with her friend, Niacey, she went to school with.

BeBe had been focused on taking care of her responsibilities, bills, car notes, and rent. She was trying to get to a bag.

Going to school and working left her with no time to herself, so she couldn't wait to turn up with her girl tonight. She walked into the basement area where the elevator awaited her.

"Excuse me, Mrs., can I get your help for a second? My daughter fell down the stairs," a man approached and said.

"Oh my god, sure." BeBe ran in her heels and dress to help the man and his daughter.

Once in the staircase, BeBe saw nobody.

"Where is she?" BeBe asked.

The man grabbed BeBe by the back of her neck, bending her over on the stairs.

"Please, nooo!" BeBe screamed before the man lifted her dress up and moved her panties to the side.

Dollar rammed his manhood into her tightness.

"Ahhhahhh, noo," Bebe cried as Dollar roughly fucked her from behind.

The stairwell door flew open.

Boc. . .

Boc. . .

Boc. . .

Boc. . .

Knight shot Dollar in his head then pushed Dollar off his little sister, who was shaking and crying. BeBe saw Knight and took his gun, then emptied the clip into Dollar's lifeless body, letting out her pain he just inflicted upon her.

Knight took BeBe outside and put her inside his car, leaving her car there. The past two days, Knight had been following Dollar, waiting for the perfect time to strike like a snake.

Knight wondered why Dollar was parked behind Patterson Projects. He saw BeBe walk into the building, but he didn't know it was his sister because she got thick and more beautiful than the last time he saw her.

He followed Dollar in the build, but Dollar went through the front way for some reason. Knight didn't know it was BeBe until she turned around and took the gun from him.

"Thank you." BeBe couldn't believe what just happened to her, and she was still a little shaky.

"I'm sorry you had to go through that." Knight felt so bad for what just happened. He wished he could have entered the build faster, but he didn't have a clue what Dollar was up to.

"Who was he?" she asked.

"The brother of someone I killed, I believe." Knight owed her his honesty after what she had just experienced, and because he felt it was his fault.

"When you got out?"

"Recently," he shot back, stopping at a red light.

"How come you ain't come see me?" BeBe hit him in his arm.

"Because I was busy. But, of course, I didn't know *you* were my parole officer."

"Whatever. But on another note, please don't tell nobody about what just happened," she said seriously, feeling ashamed and embarrassed she got raped. BeBe didn't want people to look down on her because she got raped. Especially her brothers, who she really loved.

"That's between me and you, I swear. I got you."

"Ok."

"Let's go get something to eat at that 24-hour dinner spot uptown," Knight said, hoping to catch up on old times with his sister, who he missed when he was locked up in VA.

***

Michell Projects, BX

Lil' K texted Red, telling her to hurry up so they could go to Blu's funeral. It was early in the morning. Everybody knew Lil' K wasn't a morning person, and he got real cranky.

He wore a black tuxedo for his boy's funeral. Today made him realize friends and family had more value than money and diamonds.

The skies were out and beautiful today. Lil' K loved nice days. It made the Bronx energy live for some reason. When he texted Red again telling her they were going to be late, he felt a gun to his head.

Lil' K saw the man in his car door mirror, but the man's face was new to him.

"Revenge is the sweetest thing next to pussy. You first and your brothers next. There's a new cowboy in town," the man said.

"Every dog has his day," Lil' K said.

Bloc. . .

The man shot Lil' K in his head, running off. . .

***

Red saw she had a text from Lil' K while waiting on the elevator in her mom's build. She dropped off some money to her mom before going to Blu's funeral.

Red couldn't believe Blu was gone, because outta the whole crew, he always had her back since they were kids, besides Lil' K. Even when she used to beef with Banger, her own brother, Blu would take up for her.

The gunshot from outside made her take the stairs downstairs instead of waiting on the slow elevator. Once outside, she had her gun out but saw nobody. She went to ask Lil' K what happened, who was parked across the street.

"NOOOOOO!" Red screamed, seeing a small gunshot wound to his head.

Red checked for a pulse and found one, so he was still alive. She pushed his body over into the passenger seat and rushed him to the hospital.

***

An Hour Later

The doctor told Red that Lil' K would make it, thanks to her fast response. He told her if she would have come a minute later, then most likely, he'd be dead right now.

The bullet didn't hit any parts of the brain, just tissue, because the way Lil' K had his head the moment he was shot saved his life. Tears of joy flooded Red's face. She was happy and wanted to call his brothers to tell them the news.

Outside, she called Knight first and told him. Knight stopped what he had going on and informed her he was on his way to the hospital.

When she called Kazzy Loc, he picked up on the last ring. Hearing Lil' K being shot got him heated. When Red started to tell him what hospital she was at, four men jumped out of a van, grabbing her.

The men were so big and strong, Red couldn't do anything. The little fighting she did made the men rough her little ass up more and toss her in the van.

***

Parkchester, BX

Kazzy Loc heard everything over the phone, and it sounded like Red was fighting a wrestling team. He quickly got dressed in a sweatsuit and called Knight.

"Yo," Knight answered on the other end.

"You heard what happened to Lil' K?" Kazzy asked.

"Yeah, I'm on my way to the hospital right now," Knight said.

"Somebody just snatched up Red, bro. Some crazy shit going on be—" Kazzy Loc's words were cut short when he opened his door to see six high-power assault rifles pointed at him.

"You there?" Knight asked.

"Bro, they here for me. I love you," Kazzy said before they took him and his phone.

***

Uptown, Bronx

Knight heard Kazzy Loc's phone go dead and couldn't believe his ears. Something was going down, and he planned to get to the bottom of it.

Beep. . .

Beep. . .

A big truck stopped in front of his car. The back doors opened on the truck, and Knight saw gunmen about to light his car up. He rushed out, crawling on the floor.

Tat

Tat

Tat

Tat

Tat

Tat

Knight fired a few shots back, hitting two of the gunmen with wild shots before a van hit him from behind. The impact of the van was so hard, Knight flew a couple of feet away from the van.

Five masked men grabbed Knight out the middle of the street as civilians recorded it on their iPhones. When Knight was tossed in the back, they pulled off.

***

Washington Heights, NY

Paco had been trying to call everybody, even Red, and nobody picked up their phone. Paco had to re-up. He only had ten birds left, and that ten had already been pre-ordered.

Having a little crew in Washington Heights made shit easy for him because the Heights were full of money. He walked into one of his trap builds to pick up some money from his workers.

Inside the apartment, something was off about the whole vibe, because normally, he would smell weed smoke and hear loud music.

"Fuck!" he shouted, seeing two of his people dead on the living room floor next to stacks of money and drugs.

Paco turned to leave, thinking it was a hit, because if it was a robbery, then the money and drugs would have been gone.

Once the elevator doors opened, a gang of gunmen dressed in all black tackled him to the floor, putting zip ties on his hands and ankles, carrying him off.

Paco didn't know if these were the feds, ops, or some special secret agency shit, but he played it cool. He prayed every second, asking God for forgiveness and promising to never sell drugs again if he made it out alive. Paco knew better than to promise the higher power that he would never rob again, because that would be a bold-face lie. . .

To Be Continued...
Jack Boyz N Da Hood 3
Coming Soon

Submission Guideline

Submit the first three chapters of your completed manuscript to
ldpsubmissions@gmail.com, subject line: Your book's title. The
manuscript must be in a .doc file and sent as an attachment. Document should be in Times New Roman, double spaced and in size
12 font. Also, provide your synopsis and full contact information.
If sending multiple submissions, they must each be in a separate
email.

Have a story but no way to send it electronically? You can still
submit to LDP/Ca$h Presents. Send in the first three chapters,
written or typed, of your completed manuscript to:

LDP: Submissions Dept
Po Box 944
Stockbridge, Ga 30281

DO NOT send original manuscript. Must be a duplicate.

Provide your synopsis and a cover letter containing your full contact information.

Thanks for considering LDP and Ca$h Presents.

COKE KINGS V

KING OF THE TRAP III

By **T.J. Edwards**

GORILLAZ IN THE BAY V

3X KRAZY III

De'Kari

THE STREETS ARE CALLING II

Duquie Wilson

KINGPIN KILLAZ IV

STREET KINGS III

PAID IN BLOOD III

CARTEL KILLAZ IV

DOPE GODS III

Hood Rich

SINS OF A HUSTLA II

ASAD

KINGZ OF THE GAME VI

Playa Ray

SLAUGHTER GANG IV

RUTHLESS HEART IV

By Willie Slaughter

FUK SHYT II

By Blakk Diamond

TRAP QUEEN

RICH $AVAGE II

By Troublesome

YAYO V

GHOST MOB II

Stilloan Robinson

CREAM III

By Yolanda Moore

SON OF A DOPE FIEND III

HEAVEN GOT A GHETTO II

By Renta

FOREVER GANGSTA II

GLOCKS ON SATIN SHEETS III

By Adrian Dulan

LOYALTY AIN'T PROMISED III

By Keith Williams

THE PRICE YOU PAY FOR LOVE III

By Destiny Skai

I'M NOTHING WITHOUT HIS LOVE II

SINS OF A THUG II

TO THE THUG I LOVED BEFORE II

By Monet Dragun

LIFE OF A SAVAGE IV

MURDA SEASON IV

GANGLAND CARTEL IV

CHI'RAQ GANGSTAS IV

KILLERS ON ELM STREET IV

JACK BOYZ N DA BRONX III

A DOPEBOY'S DREAM II

By **Romell Tukes**

QUIET MONEY IV

EXTENDED CLIP III

THUG LIFE IV

By **Trai'Quan**

THE STREETS MADE ME III

By **Larry D. Wright**

IF YOU CROSS ME ONCE II

ANGEL III

By **Anthony Fields**

FRIEND OR FOE III

By **Mimi**

SAVAGE STORMS III

By **Meesha**

BLOOD ON THE MONEY III

By J-Blunt

THE STREETS WILL NEVER CLOSE II

By K'ajji

NIGHTMARES OF A HUSTLA III

By King Dream

IN THE ARM OF HIS BOSS

By Jamila

HARD AND RUTHLESS III

MOB TOWN 251 II

By Von Diesel

LEVELS TO THIS SHYT II

By Ah'Million

MOB TIES III

By SayNoMore

BODYMORE MURDERLAND III

By Delmont Player

THE LAST OF THE OGS III

Tranay Adams

FOR THE LOVE OF A BOSS II

By C. D. Blue

MOBBED UP II

By King Rio

Romell Tukes

Available Now

RESTRAINING ORDER **I & II**
By **CA$H & Coffee**
LOVE KNOWS NO BOUNDARIES **I II & III**
By **Coffee**
RAISED AS A GOON I, II, III & IV
BRED BY THE SLUMS I, II, III
BLAST FOR ME I & II
ROTTEN TO THE CORE I II III
A BRONX TALE I, II, III
DUFFLE BAG CARTEL I II III IV V
HEARTLESS GOON I II III IV V
A SAVAGE DOPEBOY I II
DRUG LORDS I II III
CUTTHROAT MAFIA I II
By **Ghost**
LAY IT DOWN **I & II**
LAST OF A DYING BREED I II
BLOOD STAINS OF A SHOTTA I & II III
By **Jamaica**
LOYAL TO THE GAME I II III
LIFE OF SIN I, II III
By **TJ & Jelissa**
BLOODY COMMAS I & II
SKI MASK CARTEL I II & III
KING OF NEW YORK I II,III IV V

192

RISE TO POWER I II III

COKE KINGS I II III IV

BORN HEARTLESS I II III IV

KING OF THE TRAP I II

By **T.J. Edwards**

IF LOVING HIM IS WRONG…I & II

LOVE ME EVEN WHEN IT HURTS I II III

By **Jelissa**

WHEN THE STREETS CLAP BACK I & II III

THE HEART OF A SAVAGE I II III

By **Jibril Williams**

A DISTINGUISHED THUG STOLE MY HEART I II & III

LOVE SHOULDN'T HURT I II III IV

RENEGADE BOYS I II III IV

PAID IN KARMA I II III

SAVAGE STORMS I II

By **Meesha**

A GANGSTER'S CODE I &, II III

A GANGSTER'S SYN I II III

THE SAVAGE LIFE I II III

CHAINED TO THE STREETS I II III

BLOOD ON THE MONEY I II

By **J-Blunt**

PUSH IT TO THE LIMIT

By **Bre' Hayes**

BLOOD OF A BOSS **I, II, III, IV, V**

SHADOWS OF THE GAME

TRAP BASTARD

By **Askari**

THE STREETS BLEED MURDER **I, II & III**

THE HEART OF A GANGSTA I II& III

By **Jerry Jackson**

CUM FOR ME I II III IV V VI VII

An **LDP Erotica Collaboration**

BRIDE OF A HUSTLA **I II & II**

THE FETTI GIRLS **I, II& III**

CORRUPTED BY A GANGSTA I, II III, IV

BLINDED BY HIS LOVE

THE PRICE YOU PAY FOR LOVE I II

DOPE GIRL MAGIC I II III

By **Destiny Skai**

WHEN A GOOD GIRL GOES BAD

By **Adrienne**

THE COST OF LOYALTY I II III

By Kweli

A GANGSTER'S REVENGE **I II III & IV**

THE BOSS MAN'S DAUGHTERS I II III IV V

A SAVAGE LOVE **I & II**

BAE BELONGS TO ME I II

A HUSTLER'S DECEIT I, II, III

WHAT BAD BITCHES DO I, II, III

SOUL OF A MONSTER I II III

KILL ZONE

A DOPE BOY'S QUEEN I II

By **Aryanna**

A KINGPIN'S AMBITON

A KINGPIN'S AMBITION **II**

I MURDER FOR THE DOUGH

By **Ambitious**

TRUE SAVAGE I II III IV V VI VII

DOPE BOY MAGIC I, II, III

MIDNIGHT CARTEL I II III

CITY OF KINGZ I II

By **Chris Green**

A DOPEBOY'S PRAYER

By **Eddie "Wolf" Lee**

THE KING CARTEL **I, II & III**

By **Frank Gresham**

THESE NIGGAS AIN'T LOYAL **I, II & III**

By **Nikki Tee**

GANGSTA SHYT **I II &III**

By **CATO**

THE ULTIMATE BETRAYAL

By **Phoenix**

BOSS'N UP **I , II & III**

By **Royal Nicole**

I LOVE YOU TO DEATH

By Destiny J

I RIDE FOR MY HITTA

I STILL RIDE FOR MY HITTA

By **Misty Holt**

LOVE & CHASIN' PAPER

By **Qay Crockett**

TO DIE IN VAIN

SINS OF A HUSTLA

By **ASAD**

BROOKLYN HUSTLAZ

By **Boogsy Morina**

BROOKLYN ON LOCK I & II

By **Sonovia**

GANGSTA CITY

By **Teddy Duke**

A DRUG KING AND HIS DIAMOND I & II III

A DOPEMAN'S RICHES

HER MAN, MINE'S TOO I, II

CASH MONEY HO'S

THE WIFEY I USED TO BE I II

By Nicole Goosby

TRAPHOUSE KING **I II & III**

KINGPIN KILLAZ I II III

STREET KINGS I II

PAID IN BLOOD **I II**

CARTEL KILLAZ I II III

DOPE GODS I II

By **Hood Rich**

LIPSTICK KILLAH **I, II, III**

CRIME OF PASSION I II & III

FRIEND OR FOE I II

By **Mimi**

STEADY MOBBN' **I, II, III**

THE STREETS STAINED MY SOUL I II

By **Marcellus Allen**

WHO SHOT YA **I, II, III**

SON OF A DOPE FIEND I II

HEAVEN GOT A GHETTO

Renta

GORILLAZ IN THE BAY **I II III IV**

TEARS OF A GANGSTA I II

3X KRAZY I II

DE'KARI

TRIGGADALE I II III

Elijah R. Freeman

GOD BLESS THE TRAPPERS I, II, III

THESE SCANDALOUS STREETS I, II, III

FEAR MY GANGSTA I, II, III IV, V

THESE STREETS DON'T LOVE NOBODY I, II

BURY ME A G I, II, III, IV, V

A GANGSTA'S EMPIRE I, II, III, IV

THE DOPEMAN'S BODYGAURD I II

THE REALEST KILLAZ I II III

THE LAST OF THE OGS I II

Tranay Adams

THE STREETS ARE CALLING

Duquie Wilson

MARRIED TO A BOSS... I II III

By Destiny Skai & Chris Green

KINGZ OF THE GAME I II III IV V

Playa Ray

SLAUGHTER GANG I II III

RUTHLESS HEART I II III

By Willie Slaughter

FUK SHYT

By Blakk Diamond

DON'T F#CK WITH MY HEART I II

By Linnea

ADDICTED TO THE DRAMA I II III

IN THE ARM OF HIS BOSS II

By Jamila

YAYO I II III IV

A SHOOTER'S AMBITION I II

By S. Allen
TRAP GOD I II III
RICH $AVAGE
By Troublesome
FOREVER GANGSTA
GLOCKS ON SATIN SHEETS I II
By Adrian Dulan
TOE TAGZ I II III
LEVELS TO THIS SHYT
By Ah'Million
KINGPIN DREAMS I II III
By Paper Boi Rari
CONFESSIONS OF A GANGSTA I II III
By Nicholas Lock
I'M NOTHING WITHOUT HIS LOVE
SINS OF A THUG
TO THE THUG I LOVED BEFORE
By Monet Dragun
CAUGHT UP IN THE LIFE I II III
By Robert Baptiste
NEW TO THE GAME I II III
MONEY, MURDER & MEMORIES I II III
By **Malik D. Rice**
LIFE OF A SAVAGE I II III
A GANGSTA'S QUR'AN I II III
MURDA SEASON I II III
GANGLAND CARTEL I II III
CHI'RAQ GANGSTAS I II III
KILLERS ON ELM STREET I II III

JACK BOYZ N DA BRONX I II

A DOPEBOY'S DREAM

By **Romell Tukes**

LOYALTY AIN'T PROMISED I II

By Keith Williams

QUIET MONEY I II III

THUG LIFE I II III

EXTENDED CLIP I II

By **Trai'Quan**

THE STREETS MADE ME I II

By **Larry D. Wright**

THE ULTIMATE SACRIFICE I, II, III, IV, V, VI

KHADIFI

IF YOU CROSS ME ONCE

ANGEL I II

IN THE BLINK OF AN EYE

By **Anthony Fields**

THE LIFE OF A HOOD STAR

By Ca$h & Rashia Wilson

THE STREETS WILL NEVER CLOSE

By K'ajji

CREAM I II

By Yolanda Moore

NIGHTMARES OF A HUSTLA I II

By King Dream

CONCRETE KILLA I II

By Kingpen

HARD AND RUTHLESS I II

MOB TOWN 251

By Von Diesel

GHOST MOB II

Stilloan Robinson

MOB TIES I II

By SayNoMore

BODYMORE MURDERLAND I II

By Delmont Player

FOR THE LOVE OF A BOSS

By C. D. Blue

MOBBED UP

By King Rio

BOOKS BY LDP'S CEO, CA$H

TRUST IN NO MAN

TRUST IN NO MAN 2

TRUST IN NO MAN 3

BONDED BY BLOOD

SHORTY GOT A THUG

THUGS CRY

THUGS CRY 2

THUGS CRY 3

TRUST NO BITCH

TRUST NO BITCH 2

TRUST NO BITCH 3

TIL MY CASKET DROPS

RESTRAINING ORDER

RESTRAINING ORDER 2

IN LOVE WITH A CONVICT

LIFE OF A HOOD STAR

Romell Tukes

CPSIA information can be obtained
at www.ICGtesting.com
Printed in the USA
LVHW020026110921
697560LV00017B/1514